In the Shadow of the Deadwoods

LaTisha Redding

Library of Congress Cataloging-in-Publication available upon request.

Text Copyright © 2025 by LaTisha Redding
All rights reserved.
Printed in the United States of America
Paperback ISBN: 979-8-9878886-8-1
Ebook ISBN: 979-8-9878886-9-8
Cover design by Artscandare
Published 2025 by Gil&Wil Press, LLC
Visit: www.latisharedding.com
First Printing, 2025

CHAPTER 1

NORTH AMERICA; NORTH CAROLINA, 2054

As dusk settled across the trees and behind the walls of the Sisterhood, fifteen-year-old Haze returned to the large dwelling that she and her family shared with members of the Sisterhood.

Sometimes, the other girls needed to do these patrols. They were supposed to take turns. Haze never volunteered to do them, yet somehow, she ended up checking the gates before nightfall anyway.

Five large dwellings surrounded by an assortment of blue, purple, and yellow irises came into view. Each dwelling contained ten to fifteen rooms and housed twenty Sister-friends.

The Sister-friends ranged from babies to the ones who had lived prior to the war. The Elder Sisters had been careful not to group the women and girls according to age. Instead, the

Elder Sisters dwelled with the younger ones to show them the Sisterhood way.

When the ground warmed in spring, Haze would plant her favorite color of irises, the yellow ones, and return her potted gingerroot to the spot outside her window.

Haze pressed her hand against her empty, rumbling stomach and hoped that one of the Sister-friends had saved her some dinner. It took a lot of time to patrol the Sisterhood, and she had missed the gathering for the third evening in a row.

The trees, with their bare and knobby branches, stretched down toward her like one of the Sister-friends' arms. Gray sky with streaks of pale blue peeked through the branches like a playful child.

With one fist, Haze rubbed her left eye for the umpteenth time that day. The itching started the night before and hadn't stopped.

The raised voice of the Head Sister startled Haze as she approached from the east corner of the house.

Haze's seven-year-old brother, Hugh, twisted behind her mother's long skirt, shifting from one side of her body to the other.

The Head Sister, Phoenyx, pointed at Haze's brother, and even though Haze wasn't in hearing distance yet, she knew what they were discussing. Haze's mother folded her arms across her chest and lifted her chin against the much taller and younger woman.

Haze sped up and tried not to run toward the women. Haze's mother angled away from Phoenyx.

As Haze approached, her mother pushed Hugh toward her. Her brother hurried away from the women.

Haze grabbed his outstretched hand and hauled him toward her. Where was Sister-grandmother? Several of the other Sister-friends exited the dwelling and, although they kept their distance, circled around the women.

A sudden chill made Haze shiver. The last time she'd felt that chill, her mother had announced that her father had left and not to expect his return. That was long before their life in the Sisterhood.

Haze clutched her little brother closer to her and, side-stepping between her mother and Phoenyx, she pushed her way through the circle of women and toward the front door, where three cloth sacks were sprawled across the front of the door.

Sister-friend Harriet, the oldest of the women in their dwelling, didn't step aside, as customary when Haze approached the door. "Great afternoon to you, Sister-Harriet," Haze said, and the woman didn't budge or return the greeting.

"It took you long enough," Sister-Harriet said.

Haze replied, "The stones against the gate are too heavy. I can't lift them. I need Shaye's help. And the other girls."

"That's not what you need. What you need is some backbone. Once upon a time, I had a son your age, and he had to do the same thing. It's high time you accept that you're just as good as a boy to lift the stones. You can outwork any boy if you try. Your mother knows this as well. You should be proud."

Haze gritted her teeth. Perhaps a boy would want to lift the stones. "I pulled something in my shoulder again," she said.

Haze's grandmother and aunt pushed their way out of the door, bumping a Sister-friend with the sack thrown across their shoulders.

Haze's grandmother told her, "Pick up the sack. We're leaving."

Haze's aunt, Sister-aunt, dragged the back of her hand across her flushed and wet face. No telling how long she had been crying. Behind Sister-aunt, Haze's cousin, Jess, also crying, dumped the pile of clothes she carried onto the ground.

Some clothes belonged to Haze. Jess shook her head at Haze. Jess was half a head shorter than Haze and had a small frame. Probably won't grow taller than a ten-year-old boy, Sister-grandmother often said.

Whatever that meant, since there were no ten-year-old boys in the Sisterhood.

Behind all of them, the Sisters closed the door.

Phoenyx said to Haze's mother, "You know the rules. No males are allowed to stay in the Sisterhood over the age of six. I don't care what you say. I don't believe that this boy's only five."

Haze's brother had lost one front tooth days ago. This morning, the other tooth had popped out.

Haze's stomach tightened at the silent stares from the other Sisters. Wouldn't any of them speak out?

Haze's mother insisted, as she had for days, "I'm telling you, he's only five. How would you know a child's age, seeing that you've never had one? And likely never will."

When Haze and her family had arrived at the Sisterhood four years ago, Phoenyx wasn't old enough to cast any votes as part of the Sisterhood. It was reserved only for women twenty and over.

But when the eldest, Sister Edna, took sick, Phoenyx had stepped in, or stepped on others, as Haze's grandmother muttered, to keep the Sisterhood running smoothly. Sister Edna had died earlier that summer, and Phoenyx continued in her place.

Jess dragged a sack toward Haze. "They're sending us back into the Outerworld," Jess said with a whimper.

Haze asked her, "Where's the Sisterhood these women preach day and night?"

One of the Sisters heard her question. "That's for those who follow our beliefs. You know that," she replied. "The Outerworld is for people like your mother and your grandmother. They can't follow the rules. They are still too identified with life before the war."

Haze tightened her grip on her brother's hand.

Haze's mother wasn't much older than Haze when the war happened. The world wasn't a safe place then, according to her grandmother, but it was safer than this current world. It'd had far more people, and depending on where a woman lived, there was fresh water to drink and stores to buy food. And women traveled whenever and wherever they wanted. They had to be careful back then with some of the males.

Now, women had to be careful with all males, whether a lone male or a band of males.

The Sisters' dress billowed against the chilly wind. Phoenyx didn't wear dresses. She wore pants and had allowed all the Sisters to wear them as well.

Haze's grandmother pushed her way through the crowd until she stood in front of Phoenyx. "You're not hurting us. I used to help young women just like you. When life's good and the babies are fat, you ignore me. When life's bad and the babies die, you beg for my help. But I won't be here. And my granddaughters will have a future," she said.

Haze's grandmother was taller than the younger woman. The women of the Sisterhood had marveled that Haze's grandmother was as tall as a man. Most of the younger Sisterhood members had never seen one up close.

Phoenyx said, "That's not important. What's important is that he has to go. He can't stay here. Leave him in the forest and let him find his way. This place is for our kind, not his. Take whatever future you think you have and leave."

There was a murmur of agreement from the two Sisters who had recently arrived at the Sisterhood. Like Haze's mother and aunt, these women were actually sisters.

The first Sister, Jade, agreed that the boy's presence brought evil to the Sisterhood. Two other Sister-friends who had married one another disagreed. "He's a child. The only thing he brings is laughter, just like the girl-children."

A second shiver passed through Haze. Her little brother looked like her father, as much as she could remember. Her father hadn't found his way back to them. Why expect a child to find his way?

One of the Sister-friends kicked a sack toward Haze and Jess.

Haze let go of her brother and latched on to the sack. Her stomach rumbled from the spicy aroma of the bean soup from inside the dwelling.

Another Sister-friend lounged in the doorway with a bowl, spooning the soup, and ignored Haze's hungry stare.

Enough. Haze heaved the sack over her shoulder and said, "Sister-Mother, we can leave here. I'll seek somewhere safe. Someplace that's for all of us. You raised me to do it. I know I can."

At the dwelling across the path, three of the girls around Haze and Jess's age watched and whispered. The shells and beads woven into their hair, much like the ones in Haze's hair, flickered against the setting sun.

Haze had come to view them as true sisters, just like Jess. Yet, none of the girls moved an inch in her direction.

By this time, more of the Sisters from old to young had gathered outside their dwellings to listen.

With shaky hands, Jess wiped the tears from her face.

Haze refused to cry.

Unlike most of the girls here, she hadn't grown up in the Sisterhood. But she didn't want to leave it either. Life inside the Sisterhood was easier than being alone outside the Sisterhood—easier when the Sister-friends worked together and didn't squabble.

But what could they do? They couldn't abandon Hugh.

Her mother shook off Haze's hand and hoarsely asked Phoenyx, "Can we stay until morning? Can we have water? Or are you putting us out like garbage?"

Phoenyx's icy stare was the answer.

CHAPTER 2

At once, Sister-grandmother pulled Haze's mother away from Phoenyx before the two women scratched at each other. When Haze's mother turned around, Haze stifled a gasp at her wild-eyed expression.

Her mother quickly pulled Hugh to her and said, "Haze, get the rest of our things."

"I have our clothes," Haze replied.

Haze's mother glared at her. "You know what I mean."

Jess quickly ducked on the other side of her own mother.

"I do," Haze said, since only she was expected to do this.

"I don't," Sister-grandmother said. "You don't need to do it."

Haze swallowed and braced herself. She left her sack on the ground and returned to the entrance of the dwelling. Now, two Sister-friends, large, bony women wearing near-matching floral dresses, blocked the doorway. Haze's grandmother had made their dresses.

Haze's eye itched more as if an ant crawled across it. "I need to get our things," she said.

The first Sister-friend Mazel replied, "You have what you need. You and—"

Before Sister-friend Mazel finished her sentence, Haze rammed through them.

They grabbed at her.

But Haze slipped out of their grasp and ran down the hall to the room that she had shared with her mother and grandmother. Her Sister-aunt and Jess had shared a room with another Sister-friend.

Haze barreled into her room.

She barely had time to register the sight of her bed, stripped of blankets, and her few clothes still neatly folded in the handmade baskets.

Haze stumbled to the floor and crawled under her mother's bed. She pulled back the corner of the rug and removed a man's shirt. Her father's red and black checkered shirt that her mother had saved. She inhaled the faintest scent of pine.

The Sisterhood made it illegal to have any items from males over the age of six.

Haze felt hands wrap around one of her ankles, and before she squirmed away, a second pair of hands grabbed her other ankle. Her blouse bunched around her chest as she was dragged from under the bed.

Haze kicked away from them, yelling, "Let me alone!"

And they let go of her.

But still, Sister-friend Mazel, who was a close friend of her mother, and Sister-friend Regan loomed over her.

Haze clutched the shirt to her chest and pulled down her own blouse. Bras weren't worn in the Sisterhood, but Haze's grandmother often stitched up some for Haze and made her wear them. Like today.

Jess still didn't have to wear one.

Sister-friend Mazel glared at Haze and the flannel shirt and crisply said, "This is why you and your family have to leave."

"Did they get her? Are they fighting?" The excited chatter from the Sister-friends still outside the dwelling seeped into the room.

The Sisterhood didn't use glass in the windows, but curtains in the spring and summer and thick rug-like curtains in the winter.

"You can never be one of us. You're still contaminated by the outside," Sister-friend Mazel continued.

"And by your father," said Sister-friend Regan.

"Don't talk about my father," Haze said, although the Sisterhood were the only ones that did. Her grandmother and mother certainly didn't. Her aunt rolled her eyes if his name was mentioned.

Haze blinked away the foggy memory of his crooked front teeth, so much like her own. She mostly resembled her mother.

Two more Sister-friends entered the small room. Haze snatched Jess's faceless yarn doll from the corner of the bed, stuffing it down her shirt.

"Take her," Sister-friend Regan said to the two women.

"Don't touch me," Haze said, feeling the wall against her back. "I'm leaving."

Each woman seized Haze's arm, and Sister-friend Mazel gripped Haze by the neck.

"You've broken the rules just like your mother," Sister friend Regan said, leading the way out, as if Haze, or the other women, didn't know it.

Haze looked back upon the collage-covered wall of flowers one last time. "Let me go!" she shouted. "I can do this on my own."

The Sister-friends thrust her out of the dwelling. Haze tripped as her foot caught in the hem of Sister-friend Regan's dress. The other Sister friends helped steady Sister friend Regan, and the woman didn't tumble to the ground alongside Haze.

Haze's Sister-friends Cara and Shaye waited until the older women headed inside before speaking.

Haze grabbed Shaye's extended hand, and the girl helped pull Haze to her feet.

"Where will you go?" Cara asked. "After the forest, there's only more forest and then the Deadwoods. What's wrong with your Sister-mother? Why can she release your brother? Let the Seekers find him. They'll take him."

"No, we have to stay together," Haze said. "I can't lose anyone else in my family."

"We're your family now, too. Aren't we?" Cara asked.

Haze stuffed her father's shirt deeper into her small sack as if she didn't hear the question. What did Cara know of life outside of the Sisterhood?

Finally, Shaye said, "Stay. My Sister-mother will let you stay with us. Let your Sister-mother go her own way. Your Sister-grandmother will surely change her mind if you stay."

"My Sister-mother's way is my way," Haze said and hugged both girls to her.

Shaye pressed a small beaded pouch into Haze's hand and said, "Take this, and may our great Mother protect you."

Haze stuffed the beaded pouch beneath her father's shirt into her sack and hurried after her family.

Phoenyx and the other Sister-friends marched them towards the Sisterhood's hidden entrance to the west of the setting sun. The entrance that Haze had just checked.

With lips pulled back into a near wolf-grin, Phoenyx held the foliage-covered spiked gate entrance open.

Haze's grandmother had opposed Phoenyx coming to power when Sister Edna sickened and died. Haze suspected that Phoenyx, despite the Sisterhood's pledges of love and forgiveness for its members, had waited to extract her revenge.

The gate shut behind them with a brief clang of the gate spike clicking against the iron lever, latching the entrance closed.

A full red moon rose above the trees, checkering their shadows against the land. It wasn't quite winter yet, but still, the nights were cold. It had been four years since they had had to fare on their own.

Haze's mother said, "It's for the best. Haze has grown silly living with them." The woman's shoulders sagged just a little against the backdrop of the moon.

"I've grown strong living with them," Haze replied, tentatively touching her itching eye. "I know what to do."

"We'll end up in the Land Void," Sister-Aunt said with a tremble to her voice, placing a shaky arm around Jess.

"Again," Haze's grandmother said with a deep sigh followed by a small cough.

Jess dropped her sack to the ground and covered her face with both hands. "We're going to die out here in the Land Void."

CHAPTER 3

In the makeshift tent pitched against the craggy ground, Haze's mother shook Haze awake. Haze rolled over, shivering under the blanket she shared with Hugh. His small snores filled the tiny space, along with her grandmother's phlegmy breathing. Jess and her aunt slept on the other side of her grandmother. Haze sat up, and the cold air rushed upon her, waking Hugh.

Her mother said, "You need to collect the water before your grandmother wakes up again. See if you can find white willow to help break her fever."

"I'll have to go further than I did yesterday," Haze replied. Although, she didn't want to go further into the forest and hoped her mother would tell her not to.

Jess rustled under her blanket, twirling the lock of hair of her yarn doll around her finger.

Hugh rubbed one eye with a curled-up fist and said, "I wanna go." He let out a small cough, similar to their grandmother's.

Haze didn't dare touch her own eye.

"No," their mother said, smoothing down his rumpled shirts. "It's too cold for you. Even with these layers on."

Her grandmother coughed and said, "You didn't tell Haze that at his age. Let them take him. He wants to go. Haze shouldn't go alone. And wake Jess. It's not fit for young girls to roam this place. Get back here as quickly as you can."

"We always do," Haze replied, hesitating. She didn't want to overwork her grandmother, who had small beads of sweat across her forehead despite the cool weather. "Grandmother, I saw some new plants yesterday. If I bring them to you, can you tell me what they are?"

"Bring them," Haze's grandmother replied before she was seized by another phlegmy cough.

Once outside, Haze discovered it was lighter and colder than she'd thought. In the wee hours of the morning, the dew continued to form on the patches of grass near their tent.

Hugh and Jess poked themselves through the hidden opening strung together by ropes for their one-room shelter. Haze took the large bush leaves and dead branches and covered the opening.

This was the third shelter they'd built after leaving the Sisterhood. They'd been in this part of the land less than a week, after quickly moving once they had spotted the shelter of a scruffy-looking man and his equally scruffy and pregnant woman for the second time.

Jess stared at Haze. Or, more specifically, Haze's eye.

"I'm not a pool of water for you to gaze into," Haze said, turning away. The skin that stretched over her left eye must've spread yet again, like an ugly rash. Except the skin had crusted like a scab. And a small piece of skin protruded like a small ant bite against one eye. It had stopped itching for now.

Hugh reached up and ran his stubby finger underneath the bumpy patch of skin. "It's like a patch, Haze."

"No, it's not. And I don't need it infected," she said, pulling his hand down, which felt too warm for the weather. "Let's go north this time for water."

They had walked for days on end to move away from the Sisterhood's land. The Sisterhood had included some supplies and tools in their sacks.

With glee, Jess flashed a knife once they were out of sight of the tent. "I took it from Sister-aunt."

"You can stop calling my mom that. We're not part of the Sisterhood anymore, remember?" Haze said and dipped between the trees, which weren't as dense and full as the ones around the Sisterhood. The sandy earth had less weight to its soil. This place had less of everything and made it difficult to glean the water from plants.

"I still can't believe they put us out of the Sisterhood," Jess said. She playfully swatted Hugh on the shoulder. "Little boy, if you hadn't lost your front teeth—"

"I'd rather have my brother than the Sisterhood," Haze said, wondering why Jess would say such things with Hugh listening.

As if Hugh sensed the same thing, he scampered away.

"I miss the Sisterhood. Don't you? Our mothers and grandmother can keep Hugh," Jess said, seizing Haze by the arm and dug her nails into the flesh. Her voice tremored. "We can go back."

"You should go back. You cry every night when you think they're asleep," Haze said, staying perfectly still despite the sting from Jess's nails.

For a moment, Jess seemed to think it over. "We better find that white bark stuff. And something to eat," she said, releasing her grip on Haze.

Haze rubbed her arm and spied a cluster of oyster mushrooms at the base of a standing dead oak tree. She unsheathed her small knife. "We'll have breakfast today."

Hugh ran back to her, holding a thick stick. "Look at this. It's a knife. No, a sword," he said and swung it around as if some invisible person stood in front of him.

The Sisterhood wouldn't let any of the boys even point a stick and pretend it was a weapon. Those who were caught were punished with no food for the day. Hugh had gone without food at least once a week. No matter, her mother had still snuck it to him.

As Haze continued to look upon her brother, her mind filled with the image of Hugh. And not just the sight but she heard it as well, as if it happened right in front of her now. Hugh in the woods alone at night struggling to find food and water for himself. Or was he alone? Because he turned with his head tilted up, as if speaking to someone.

Jess lightly punched her in the arm and said, "Quit daydreaming."

"I'm not," Haze said, rubbing her still sore arm and wished her cousin would be silent. "Wait, where's Hugh?"

She pivoted in a half-circle.

Jess pointed to the foliage up ahead. "Told you to stop daydreaming," she said.

Haze dashed ahead before Hugh wandered too far or fell and hurt himself or a million other things that could happen to him, according to her mother. Hugh had gone down a sandy slope and examined an old, large round piece of rubber.

"Look Haze. It's a...a tire," he shouted up at her moments before the shrub-like trees in the distance moved.

Haze froze inside and motioned for him to come back up the slope. But Hugh didn't see her motions. He had already turned back to his new toy and attempted to set it upright and roll it.

She hissed his name. "Hugh!"

Hugh's eyes opened wide.

He let go of the tire and bounded up the slope towards her.

Two males burst from the shrubs.

Haze held in a scream. She grabbed Hugh's outstretched hand and ran.

Her brother was a fast enough runner.

Haze ran faster and felt his small hand slip out of hers.

One of the males was right behind them.

Haze barreled through the trees, not wanting to lead them to Jess or back to their shelter. She pivoted west, knowing that if they followed her, they'd miss Jess.

Haze glanced over her shoulder. Despite the distance that had been between her and the males when she started, the first one had nearly closed that distance. Where was the other one?

"Hugh. Hide," she said. The words almost stuck in her throat, which felt as if it were closing.

They ran through a cluster of trees. Hugh dropped and rolled himself under a bush as the Sisterhood had taught the little children to do.

Haze ran several more feet and ducked behind a tree.

There was nothing but an open field ahead. The males would surely see them.

The footsteps of the first male stopped.

Haze didn't dare peek out from her hiding spot. But from her spot, she saw Jess, who was also hiding up in a tree about fifty feet away. Jess held her small yarn doll clamped between her teeth, as if to stifle her screams. Had Jess seen them coming? Haze locked eyes with her cousin. Jess hadn't given the warning of someone approaching by making a mock bird call.

Jess removed the yarn doll and mouthed, "I'm sorry."

Hugh's angry and frightened cry cut through what was left of the morning mist. "Let go! Let me go!" Hugh shouted, followed by a spurting cough.

The first male called to her, "Come out. We have him."

Haze's heart sank, and her slightly bumped eye felt as if it had sand in it. She peered around the tree, and the man held Hugh upside down by his legs.

Her brother flailed his arms helplessly.

When Haze turned back, the second male was in front of her. She jolted against the tree.

He had been there all along.

CHAPTER 4

The wet earth clung to her shoes as Haze flew at the first male, clawing for her brother. "Put him down. Let go of him."

Still dangling by his legs, Hugh coughed hard toward the male that held him upside down.

The second male easily pushed Haze away yet said, "The boy's sick. Drop him."

Hugh stopped moving. The first male roughly dropped Hugh, who still didn't move. His small body thudded to the ground, landing on his back. They continued to stand over him.

Haze inched towards her brother, still eyeing the men. "Hugh?"

"He can't answer you. Got some sort of fever," the first male said.

"I don't like to see it," the second male said. "We can't leave him."

Haze made to snatch Hugh up but didn't want to get too close to the males. She still had her tiny knife and palmed it.

"Don't do it," the second male said to her with a sigh.

Haze was still small when her father left. She didn't know if all males were the height of these two and as well-fed.

The two men were joined by a younger male, all dressed in similar black gear from head to boot-covered foot.

The younger male briefly stopped at the sight of her and, like the two other men, initially cocked his head. Haze stared back hard, willing the slight bump on her left eye to shrink so she could see him fully.

Then, he seemed to forget she existed.

***

For three days, Haze journeyed beside them, along with her silent and sickly little brother as they pushed deeper and deeper into an area filled with sand dunes. They all spoke the same language, and the men didn't appear to have any fear of her listening.

Haze hadn't heard the voice of an adult man since she was Hugh's age and had no desire to speak. They didn't speak much, either.

If they planned to rape her and kill her, they would've done that already. They hadn't—and she could almost hear the Sisterhood whisper in the wind—not yet.

And these men had food.

The first man, Ollie—the one who had seized Hugh—now passed her brother a stick with a hunk of meat impaled on it fresh from the fire spit.

Ollie passed Haze a portion too, and she hungrily tore into it.

"So she ate it this time? Better give her some more," Ollie said. "She's 'bout ready to gnaw her paw off."

A round of chuckles bubbled through the small circle of men around the fire. Hugh crawled closer to the flames, and Haze pulled him back.

Another round of chuckles surfaced. Haze sat back on her hunches and regarded the men over the fire.

"You can't speak, girl?" The second man asked. The other two called him Roy. A splattering of gray whiskers poked out of his chin.

"She does, but only to her brother," the youngest of the three, Ty, replied.

Something about him seemed familiar, and his gaze held no malice. He shoved the last bit of meat into his mouth and folded his somewhat gangly legs under him.

Ollie held a tin cup under her nose. Haze turned her head away. Let them drink the water or whatever liquid sloshed in the cup they passed around.

"Forget it. She takes what she can from the leaves in the morning," Ollie said.

Hugh snatched the cup and, tilting back, emptied it into his mouth. Haze wanted to kick him.

She met the solemn eyes of Ty across the fire, and a mist seemed to rise out of the flames and shape itself into the form of three men—and not one of the men in the vision appeared like the three in front of her. The vision of the three men disappeared as quickly as it had materialized.

"What's wrong with you, girl? Why're you stretching your eye like that?" Roy asked.

"And what's wrong with your other eye?" Ollie added as he reached over and, with one calloused fingertip, barely touched her face.

Haze kicked at him wildly. "Don't touch me."

"Haze," Hugh said with a whimper and rolled to his feet. He seemed unsure of whether to run and hide.

Haze quickly jumped to her feet, but Roy, gray whiskers or not, was faster.

"Best keep your hands to yourself," Ollie said. "We know who'll handle her."

"All right, Darlin'," Roy said, pulling her back into a sitting position. "Settle down."

Ty rose and kicked sand over the already smoldering fire. "Let's move from here. If we push on, we'll get to the gate before Hal drinks himself to sleep. That way, Haze," and he seemed to check her reaction as he said her name, "and her brother can sleep in a bed."

"Let us go and we can sleep where we please," Haze said, struggling to keep down the food she'd just eaten. "Why won't you tell me where you're taking my brother? How many times can you hear the same question without answering?"

"We've told you. You're free to leave," Ollie said.

"I'm not leaving without my brother! He's done nothing to you. Who knows what you'll do to him. What kind of men are you?" Haze asked, rubbing her bruised arms. She had already attacked Roy earlier that day and had been repeatedly thrown to the ground.

The men remained silent.

Her brother's skin was hot and damp when he tried to crawl into Haze's lap. "I don't feel good," he said.

Haze cuddled him and said, "I'll find you some—"

Hugh whimpered as Ty pulled him away with one deft move. Ollie and Roy rose and helped Ty stamp out the fire.

***

During the night's trek, Haze's hands and feet felt like cold bricks while she wondered what would become of her grandmother. Was her mother out searching for her? Well, of course she was, and especiallyHugh. Did her auntie stay with her grandmother while her mother and Jess searched for her?

Hugh finally tired, and Ollie and Roy took turns carrying him on their backs. Haze used her hair to dab at her own hot and damp forehead.

The darkness still enveloped them, and the sand grew thinner when Haze made out something rather large and solid in the distance.

She wanted to ask what it was, but she was afraid to speak to the men again. And she didn't have to because soon thereafter, they approached a massive gate made of cinderblocks.

Haze touched the cold stone. The Sisterhood had nothing like this, and it was exactly what they needed.

The five men already at the gate let them in by swinging open the cinderblock door attached to massive hinges that glinted against the dark.

When the first gatekeeper saw Haze, he let out a long whistle that raised the hairs on her neck. Like the Sisterhood, he had a lantern and held it up to get a good look at her.

The whistle stopped short when the man squinted at her angry face.

"Back to work, Hal," Ollie said.

"Right," Hal said, grunting out the word. He ambled back to the gate with the lantern.

Still, the moon illuminated some type of houses or structures further in, but this area itself was a field directly behind the gate. The sand and silty earth had stopped miles ago, and the earth felt solid again.

"Take her to the bunkhouse," Roy said.

With her hands still bound, Haze tried to lift her still unconscious brother from Ty's arms. Her arms trembled from the effort.

Ty sidestepped her and said, "Your brother stays with us."

Chapter 5

Haze woke before dawn. The barest edge of the sun glided against the wooden walls inside the bunkhouse. The dark wood had a peculiar scent, like fresh earth mingled with mint. The ceilings were almost twice the height of the Sisterhood's interior rooms. The light whistle of wind didn't penetrate the windows.

Haze breathed deeply but held in her sigh, least the women realize she was awake. She glimpsed the glass in the window frames and blinked, unsure if her vision was correct.

Once upon a time, she had seen houses with glass, but that was before she'd lived in the Sisterhood.

Wherever these men had led her, they had roomed her with three other women. But, here, there was no fire to make or water to gather, so she remained in bed waiting for them to leave.

She needed to find Hugh. Find out if he was still sick. And even if he was, they needed to leave this place.

Surely, Jess had told her mother what had happened. Her grandmother had been waiting on the white willow.

"They brought her a few days ago," the first woman whispered. "She was sick as a dog. They fetched some herbs from Millie for her. She's been knocked out since then. But she was tossing and turning last night, like someone was chasing her in her sleep."

"I heard her too. She's a noisy little thing. Sounds young," said the second woman, with a voice that sounded as if she had a stuffy nose.

"I haven't gotten a good look. She is young, though," said the first woman.

"That'll serve her well."

Haze stiffened under the cover. What would serve her well? The Sisterhood had warned of the rape and murder of women by bands of men, but they hadn't warned Haze of these types of women.

Haze peered at the two women from the flicker of light through the window. Both appeared around her mother's age, although the second one had a roundness to her that Haze had never seen on any woman.

A light yawn from the bed next to her and a ruffling of the blankets meant the third woman was awake as well.

"I saw her," said the third woman. "She's real pretty but has a messed-up eye."

In the silence that followed, Haze sensed that the women looked over at her bed. Haze was grateful the covers were over her head. Shortly after that discussion, they left.

Haze quickly threw off the covers and almost didn't see her freshly washed and neatly folded clothes at the foot of the bed.

Instead, she wore some sort of thick, flannel pants and a top. Haze immediately stripped them off and put on her own clothes.

She bumped against the tiny table with a bowl that held a few ounces of water and some small cloths and used them to wipe her face.

"You might as well put them back on. You'll wear them eventually," said third woman from in the bed across from Haze. She rolled onto her side and propped herself up on one elbow. "I'm Kacy."

The lightness of Kacy's voice meant she wasn't much older than Haze.

Haze put on her near-worn boots. The rugs, made of some sort of animal fur, tickled her feet.

"You don't have a name?"

"Haze."

"Your eye doesn't look that bad. Haze."

When the door opened, Kacy immediately lay down and shut her eyes.

An older woman glided into the room, bracelets jingling on her wrists. Haze instinctively rubbed the scabs on her wrists. Roy had finally cut the ropes off her before she entered the bunkhouse the other night.

The woman eyed Haze carefully as she spoke. "I'm Iris, and I'm here to make sure you get something to eat and show you around."

Haze stared at her. The woman's lips were painted a deep red, and her eyelids shimmered with gold.

"Come now," Iris said, eyeballing the untouched clothes still on Haze's bed.

"I have a brother," Haze said. "Where is he? Can you take me to him?"

"I'm sure your brother's doing just fine," she said and seemed almost afraid to touch Haze, and her smile didn't reach her eyes.

Haze followed her outside.

This bunkhouse sat between two other bunkhouses, each equally spaced apart. The size of the other two bunkhouses dwarfed this one. It reminded Haze of the Sisterhood's dwellings. Except the Sisterhood's dwellings had more color to them. All the bunkhouses had a small bed of flowers in front.

"Are there more women in those dwellings?" Haze asked.

Iris's gold-shimmered eyes widened for a moment and she said, "No that's for the men. So, we're the Freemen's society—"

Haze cut her off and asked, "Free man?"

Iris took a deep breath and continued, "We're the Freemen's society, and we started here right after The Destruction. The Freemen have built this community to protect us women and children from the atrocities that happened during The Destruction."

Haze's sore eye watered.

These men had chased her down and captured Hugh. Refused to let him go and forced her to follow along. Yet this society was to protect children? Haze's grandmother had told her and Jess of some of the atrocities usually when Hugh wasn't around.

A handful of men jostled out of the first bunkhouse. They laughed and pushed one another until they saw Haze. Their movements slowed as some glanced in her direction and others caught sight of her and never looked away, even turning around and walking backwards.

"Goodness, honey, don't cry," Iris said, tentatively reaching out and patting Haze's shoulder for a few seconds before twirling a beaded lock of Haze's hair around her finger and then snatching her hand back.

"I'm not. I don't cry."

"Of course." A smile slid back onto the woman's face, and she said, "Those beads in your hair are like jewels. They're just dazzling in this light. Who taught you to make your hair like this? Where are you from?"

"The forest," Haze replied, careful not to even mention the Land Void.

A man and two women passed them on the path, and the two women hesitantly smiled at Haze. They stopped when she didn't return their smiles.

The Freemen's society contained far more members than the Sisterhood.

As Iris chattered away about their history, she led Haze on the east side of the community. This place appeared to be some sort of old military base.

The Sisterhood had insisted on teaching the girls the history before The War, which these Freemen called The Destruction. Now, Haze wished she'd listened more about how that way of life had disappeared.

Iris stopped in front of a circular building and squared her shoulders, as if bracing herself against some invisible force. But that lasted for only a moment. A deep sigh poured out of her and she relaxed again.

If not for the woman's exaggerated movements, Haze would've missed the sneaky corner of the eye gaze. She swept Haze's clothing from head to foot again.

"What is this place?" Haze asked suspiciously.

"You know you couldn't have come at a better time," she said. When she smiled this time, her eyes lit up, and she was almost breathless with excitement. "This is the time that the Freemen are open to new members. In another week, it'll be over."

Haze bolted.

CHAPTER 6

She didn't have to look back. Iris's squawk of outrage followed her. Haze ran, not sure where to go and trampled through what was left of a flower garden.

"Where are you going?" Iris shouted.

"To find my brother," Haze said and zigzagged around the different houses and out of Iris's sight. She barely remembered the direction of the gate she'd entered with those three guards. Was that west? It couldn't be east because that was where Iris picked her up. A little girl watched from a doorway, with her fingers in her mouth.

Haze tore past a small wooden fence no higher than her knees. Someone's already harvested vegetable garden.

She spotted a field and headed for it. She lost herself in the long-plucked stalks of corn and kneeled to the ground to catch her breath. No one followed her. Good.

Or maybe not. A dog barked nearby.

The Sisterhood had dogs, too, until earlier this year. Then, they all died from drinking the bad rainwater, which also killed the Sisterhood's crops. The dog barked again, and this time it was closer. Haze kept low and crawled to a better spot, peeking between the stalks. The dog's loud barking ricocheted through her ears as it closed in.

Haze stood.

Ollie and Roy watched from the outskirts of the field with Iris. The dog bounded up to her, tail wagging. Ollie waved her over as if she were an old friend.

She slowly made her way to the three of them.

When Ollie and Roy saw her clothes, they both turned to Iris with questioning eyes. Iris's ever-ready smile reappeared.

"You're going to meet our Freemen leaders today," Ollie said.

"Are you sure you want to stay in that...attire?" Iris asked, and now the woman examined not just Haze's clothes but her slightly veiled eye.

"Yes," Haze said. As long as her clothes were clean, she had no idea why she needed to care about her clothes to see their leaders. She'd spoken with Sister-friend Edna and Phoenyx many times in these same clothes.

Ollie and Iris exchanged glances, and each wore a strained expression afterwards. The dog barked impatiently and pulled Roy away.

Haze's stomach growled louder than the dog. She pressed her hand into her belly. She hoped she wouldn't have to carry Hugh out of this place. Right now, she didn't have the energy.

Iris snapped her fingers and said, "You know, I just realized this sweet young lady hasn't had a thing to eat." It truly seemed as if the thought had just occurred to her. "You must be ready to faint."

Haze nodded and played along. Every item Iris wore accented something about her, whether her eyes, her lips, her shoulders, her legs.

Ollie added, "I saw your brother earlier, and he's a handful. He'll fit right in here. Bet he can't wait to see ya now that we've gotten that fever out of him. And you."

"Can I get those clothes after I eat?" Haze asked, and Iris's smile made Ollie pause as if he'd never seen it before and then excused himself.

***

Back inside the bunkhouse, Iris sprayed something in the air from a small container and waved her arms around.

Haze struggled to get comfortable in the scratchy dress. It was too tight on her hips and waist. She wore dresses in the Sisterhood, cool-loose fitting dresses for the warm seasons.

Iris groaned and flung Haze's dirty clothes to the floor as if they were stained with blood.

Kacy had made up her bed and left. Haze's bed was also made up, and she wondered if Kacy did that too. Her grandmother had done that all the time.

Haze rubbed her bare arms and tried to picture Jess, her grandmother, her mother, all of them, but nothing came to her. Her grandmother could use a bed like this to sleep in.

The bunkhouse, like many of the houses that she'd seen, had glass in the window.

She twisted her arms to zip up the dress but couldn't reach the zipper. When she turned around, Iris quietly watched her with no smile.

But she immediately showed all her teeth seconds later and said, "I'll help you with that. Doesn't look like you've ever worn one of these before."

Something about this woman reminded Haze of Phoenyx. "I haven't," she said, and pretended to search for the shoes to get away from Iris.

"Well, where are you from, honey? Did you grow up out there in the woods all by your lonesome? Just you and your little brother?"

"We did," Haze said, hoping that Hugh had followed their grandmother's instruction — don't tell strangers about his family—don't tell anyone. Her father used to tell her that, too. But Hugh was barely on foot tumbling about when he left, so he never heard it from him. Her toes felt crunched in the weird shoes. Didn't they have some sort of sandal?

"That's why this is the perfect place for you. Come now, let's go."

Haze hobbled forward a few times until she got the hang of the shoe.

"I guess you won't be running away with those on," Iris said, handing Haze a coat that didn't fit quite right.

Outside the bunkhouse, two young girls planted a different flower garden, and they reminded Haze of the girls in the Sisterhood. Five or six little boys raced past her and Iris.

"Where are they going?" Haze asked, not seeing her brother with them. Was Hugh really okay?

"Nowhere. They're just playing. Now, let's get you over to the Sanctuary. It looks like it's about to rain."

On the way to the Sanctuary, the entire time, Haze kept watch for sight of Hugh. Iris had casually wound her arm through Haze's as they strolled.

Haze suspected the woman had a strong grip underneath all the fluff.

Iris pointed across the field and said, "The married couples stayed on the other side of the field. Most of the singles stayed on this side so they can get to know one another."

Something on Iris's hand glinted against the pale yellow sun.

Iris wore a ring. A wedding ring.

Haze's grandmother wore one too, although Haze's grandfather had passed during The Destruction. No other woman in the Sisterhood wore a wedding ring. Haze's mother had never had one.

For the few women that coupled, they exchanged necklaces or bracelets.

"Your ring is pretty," Haze said.

Iris held up her hand and said, "When I married, I was practically your age....and how old are you?"

"Thirteen," Haze lied.

"And that was my guess," Iris said and stroked Haze's hair, pulling some of it towards Haze's face to drape down over her eye.

From the outside, the Sanctuary had the same appearance as the bunkhouse.

Inside, the brown wood gleamed against windows that went nearly from the ceiling to the floor. About ten to twelve men moved an enormous table that had to seat about forty people.

Haze stepped back and onto Iris's foot. Iris nudged her forward. The men continued working as if she wasn't there, and she relaxed just a little.

Iris led her into an adjoining room with another group of men. But whatever discussions they were having stopped. The men parted until Haze stood directly before three men.

The first two men wore gear no different from the rest of the men she'd seen.

The third man, chubbier than the other two, wore a long, loose-fitting coat. The thickened skin over Haze's eye tingled, and she remembered her vision of the three men.

The first man said, "So you want to be part of the Freemen society?"

CHAPTER 7

For a moment, Haze considered saying no. But over the man's shoulder, Iris gave a slight nod. Haze struggled to breathe in the room, with its bricked walls and pinecone-smelling furniture.

These men, much like the guards, were well-fed. No gauntness to their cheeks or shadows beneath their eyes.

She found her voice and said, "Yes. I need help. Every year, it grows colder and harder to live in the forest."

Her words pleased the first man. "My name's Clint," he said, "and this man to the right of me is Wes."

Haze limply shook each man's hand.

The third man didn't wait for Haze to finish shaking hands. He stepped closer to her, and she felt his breath on her cheek as he scrutinized her from head to toe. "What's wrong with your eye?" he asked.

"Myles..." Clint said.

Iris had positioned herself again, in Haze's sight, over the bow-legged man's shoulder. She didn't move her head this time, but her pained expression was enough.

Haze said, "Some bug bit me while I was sleeping."

"What insect is that? I know of no such critter with the ability to create a hood over the eye. And I don't like the look of it," he said, and swept his arm around pointing to the windows, the furniture, everything in the room. "We've taken years to build our community. It can all be destroyed with a single lie. So we are careful. We don't just permit anyone to join. Especially a girl seer. Boys are meant to be seers. Only we can handle it."

"A seer? What is that?" she asked. For him not to like the looks of it, he hadn't taken his eyes off her.

Myles's arm shot out from his side, as if shielding Wes and Clint from his words. "A seer is a male with the gift of foresight. He sees events before they happen."

"In order to warn the people," Clint said, stepping away from Myles' outstretched arm. "So the seer helps protect his people."

"I'm not a seer," Haze said, backing away from the strange, bow-legged man. Her grandmother had told her about seers years ago but called it something else. Whatever it was, Haze wanted no part of it. "Is it true that this society protects women and children?" she asked.

"Yes." Clint, Wes, and Myles said in unison.

Wes said, "Myles, this young lady came here to meet us. Not be grilled about her eyes. Please pardon my comrade," he said to Haze. "As our holy man, he knows better."

Myles, the holy man, narrowed his already too-small eyes at Haze, and there was nothing holy about his gaze.

Haze tugged her coat closed and folded her arms across her chest.

Clint cleared his throat and, taking Haze by the shoulder, guided her over to the giant windows.

The nearest window pointed east, and Clint said, "From here, you can see the new home I'm building for my family. Do you have any family? Sisters, perhaps?"

He folded his hands behind his back.

"My father's dead. But my little brother's here. Can I see him?" she asked.

Clint nodded. "The guards told us about your brother. He'll fit right in here. When you have time, I'll introduce you to my wives and children."

"Wives," Haze repeated. Not sure she'd heard him correctly. All the men wore wedding rings.

"I have two," Clint said, "you'll find here that family is the foundation of the Freemen society. You've cared for your brother, so you understand that."

Haze sensed that he was genuinely pleased about that.

Clint continued, "I have five boys and two more on the way. No daughters, though. My wives could use some help."

Iris finally said, "Ollie told me that her brother's been very well-cared for, and he even knows how to read. That must've been a lot of responsibility for a Thirteen-year-old. How about I get her settled with Amie? I saw Lily this morning, and she said she doesn't want to wait another week. She's ready to have that baby now."

Myles said, "Perhaps you should think twice about that."

"I can help," Haze said quickly. Especially since she needed to avoid whatever plans Myles had already formed.

"Wonderful," Iris said with a clap. "I'll take you there now."

***

The western part of the community had dwellings larger than anything Haze had seen within the Sisterhood's land or anywhere. A makeshift flag flapped against the wind.

Each dwelling had a half a field of space between them. The actual homes had flat roofs, and on one of them, two boys and a girl peered down at her from the roof.

Further behind the dwellings and across the field, three guard towers sprouted from the earth. Men and women and older kids packed the fields, harvesting the last of the crops before true frost hit.

"We have several storehouses and smoke houses," Iris said, with her chin tilted up. She took Haze to the dwelling furthest down at the end, and a petite woman with soft brown eyes waddled out to meet them.

Before Iris or Haze spoke, the woman smothered Haze in a hug, and said, "I'm Lily."

Haze immediately stiffened. Some women of the Sisterhood liked to hug a lot, too, and she avoided them. The woman's belly pressed into Haze's side until Haze started to squirm before Lily finally let go.

"Let's go inside and show you around," Lily said.

Iris didn't stick around for the tour. And Lily didn't give her much of a tour. Mostly, she introduced her to the boys and the other wife, Amie, who was heavily pregnant.

Of the children, the oldest boy was about eight or nine and slightly taller than Hugh. He belonged to Clint and Amie.

Exhausted by nightfall, Haze had to wait for Iris to escort her back to the bunkhouse or anywhere away from the watchful wives. But Iris didn't pick her up. Instead, Lily opened the door to Ty. Haze unwrapped the three-year-old boy's arms from around her legs.

The boy had barely let go of her all afternoon while Amie napped.

Haze half-hobbled, half-hurried past Lily despite the woman's peculiar expression, which shifted back to Ty. Amie prepared dinner and had already said her goodbye.

"Everyone's having a meal by the firepit," Ty said.

"We need her back here bright and early tomorrow," Lily said to Ty.

"Of course," he replied.

Chapter 8

Once they went halfway down the road and Lily and the children appeared small, like toy soldiers, Ty asked her, "Do you like it here so far?"

"I almost can't believe that this place exists," she said, while judging him to be about eighteen years old. She'd been so frightened and so hungry when she first saw him that she hadn't noticed. "Why did you bring me here? And my little brother, who I haven't seen. I saw him born, you know. I helped deliver him."

"For your own safety. You were alone," he said, with the same solemness that he'd shown outside of the Freemen society.

"I was—" She closed her mouth so quickly that her teeth clicked.

"Your eye looks better."

Yet yours are so sad, she wanted to say.

Haze had noticed earlier that her scab of skin had shrunk a little when she saw her reflection in the sink water before she had to bathe Amie's baby. The sink in the bunkhouse had no water faucet, and neither did this one.

But Lily had a small barrel of water in the corner of the kitchen. Haze had seen her give each of the kids a cup.

The chorus of laughter from the younger kids playing in the fields almost made Haze smile. Her grandmother and her mother loved to hear babies and children laugh.

"Were you born here?" Haze asked.

Ty said, "Most everyone was. We're selective with our members."

Over and over, they passed a cluster of two or three homes similar to Clint's.

Also, over and over, the temperature dropped, and the chill penetrated her light coat. Jess would like this coat. The wind brought the smell of barbeque, which wafted towards her.

He continued, "You'll get used to it here. No woman born here has ever left. No girl either."

"And the boys? There's a lot of you."

"And that's why no girl has ever left." He seemed to permit himself a momentary smile and said, "They've already set up."

Haze didn't know how many people lived within the Freemen's walls, but she guessed that at least half of them must've milled around the firepits.

Three large firepits shot flames and spit embers into the night air, and someone played some kind of music.

The tables surrounded the firepits with handfuls of men and their many wives and children on one side of the firepit. The other side also had tables with men and their wives and children. Lines of men jammed into the last two tables with not a woman or girl in sight.

Each table had a roasted animal on it, whether a chicken or a hog.

Ty maneuvered to a table with a roasted deer on a platter and metal plates stacked nearby. Not one table had a cup.

From a nearby table, Kacy motioned Haze and Ty over. Haze picked her way through the crowd, and Kacy scooted over and made room.

"I see you've found a new friend," Kacy said. And Haze wasn't sure if it was Ty she spoke to or not.

"Where've you been? What do you do here all day?" Haze asked. She didn't hunt or dig for roots. Kacy had no callouses on her fingers unlike Haze.

Ty heaped food onto his plate, and she took as much as her plate would hold. She shoveled the still hot meat into her mouth almost as fast as Ty and barely savored the smoked flavor.

"Helping these women. Same as you. It's not too bad." Kacy said and held out her arms, revealing faded scars and a walnut-sized burn mark. "Beats scraping by on my own."

"Are you from here too?" Haze asked, noting that Kacy's scar was about six-months-old.

"Nah," Kacy said and pushed the plate of food away. She seemed in no hurry to eat it. "I came a few years back with my sister. Then I left. But I came back and discovered she'd gotten married and all of that. Big belly and all."

"Is she here? Or did she have to stay home like the ones I was with?" Haze asked.

Kacy paused and said, "She just died this quarter. Giving birth. I got to spend time with her before that though." She skimmed over her shoulder at the small group of men in back of them.

Haze dropped the food back onto her plate, picked it up and dropped it again. The Freemen had far more things than the Sisterhood and no woman in the Sisterhood lost their baby or their life. She asked, "Did the baby live?"

Kacy continued, "You're lucky that you came when you did. During the 3rd thirteen weeks of the year, they let in new members. That ends in six days. Right Ty?"

"I don't believe in luck. Or fate," Ty said, finally emptying his plate. "But I believe in good timing. Haze, I see your brother."

Haze whipped around and spotted Hugh play fighting with a boy about his age by the table with the most girls. She left Ty and Kacy without a thought and went over to him.

Hugh saw her coming and ran to her, throwing his arms around her.

"Hugh!" Haze lifted him and swung him around for just a second.

"Put me down," he said, wriggling out of her embrace. "I'm not a baby."

Haze almost dropped him. He'd never said that to her before. To some of the women in the Sisterhood, yes. Even their grandmother once. But not her.

"Tell her how you've grown taller since you've been here," Ty said over his shoulder and tossed the plates into a large barrel almost overflowing with plates.

"A lot taller," Hugh said, pointing to a nearby boy with a gapped tooth grin. "Almost as tall as Bones. He's my new friend."

You don't have time for friends, Hugh. And neither do I, she wanted to tell him. Instead, she asked, "Where did they take you? Who are you staying with?"

Hugh shrugged. "All the other boys in a bunch of big rooms. Kind of like the Sisterhood. Except it's not all girls all the time," he said, dragging out the words all the time as if he was tired and needed a nap.

"Hugh, shush. Don't talk about them," she said as Ty returned.

Haze guided Hugh back over to their table with a large bowl of fruit and some sort of bread. Kacy continued staring into the fire. Haze left her alone. She was probably thinking about her sister.

Haze wondered what her mother had done once Jess told her what happened. Was her grandmother even sicker? Did they make a fire to warm them at night? The cold season would cover the land soon. The people laughed and danced and the firepit smoldered. None of them had to worry about their families.

Haze took Hugh by the hand and said to Ty's questioning eyes, "He needs to go, you know."

Hugh didn't resist either, even though he must have known she was lying because his small face clouded over.

She moved as casually as possible with Hugh and swayed to the music just a little as she passed the dancing peo-ple. Once she cleared the area, she moved with more speed. "Hugh, let's go."

"Where?" he asked and pulled back, dragging his feet. Haze yanked him hard. Other people arrived on the path, and Haze stopped, pulling him.

"Back to Sister-mother, Sister-grandmother, Jess, and Sister-aunt. We can't stay here. This isn't our home," she said, forgetting that she had dropped those terms months ago.

Hugh looked confused and said, "Sister-mother doesn't have a home either."

"That's not what I mean. Just follow me," she snapped, pulling him a few feet more along the path. Something about this place made him behave like this because he never had before.

"Are you lost, darlin'?" a man asked from the darkness of a nearby tree.

Haze jolted. "No. My brother's—he's sick."

Hugh stopped struggling.

"Looks pretty healthy the way he's fighting with you."

Haze recognized him as the guard named Trent that had worked in the Sanctuary earlier that day. Before she could answer, a large orange flame shot up and licked the air farther across the fields, once, twice, three times. The music stopped.

"They're having another barbeque?" Hugh asked.

Trent abandoned his spot by the tree, ran down the path, and headed toward the field. A cluster of men and a handful of women also ran across it, heading towards the fire. Ty ran down the path towards her with Kacy and said, "You need to get back."

Chapter 9

"This way," Kacy said, as a wave of girls and boys surged by them.

This time, Hugh didn't try to pull away when Haze took him by the arm.

The smell of the new fire blanketed the scent of barbeque as several other girls moved alongside them. Ty, like the other men, disappeared into the fields.

"What happened?" Haze asked, while a mother with her children pushed past them. And then another crop of children stampeded past.

"I don't know, but it's not good," Kacy replied.

"Where's Ty going?" she asked. In the three days that she'd been forced to travel alongside him, Ollie, and Roy, she assumed he was more of the hunting-for-food-type.

"To make sure we're still safe," Kacy said, pointing out a nearby stick to Hugh. He ran to the nearby bushes and grabbed it.

"It's some captives," a girl behind them said. Taller than Haze and more womanly shaped, as her grandmother would say, she had been the one dancing the most at the barbeque. "Of course, they attacked us during our celebration of the holy birthday of Myles."

"Slow down, Camryn," Kacy said to the girl. "Haze is new here and doesn't know her way yet."

"Who're the captives?" Haze asked, and had she known that this was to celebrate Myles, she'd have left the event even earlier. Or not go at all.

"The bad people," Hugh said and swung the stick in front of him as if hitting an invisible foe.

"How do you know about them, Hugh?" she asked.

"All the men know about them," Hugh replied, and he twisted around to see the fire since it now appeared in back of the group. "Ty's going to get them."

When did he become such a fan of Ty? What had happened to Hugh in the day or so that they'd been here?

"He's right," Camryn said, pointing to a second fire that erupted. "That's over near our gates. That's the south wall and the first one is by the east wall. I don't know how they got in or if they got in, but I hope we get them. We're in here and free and they're captives out there. They just want to take over and ruin the place and make it a hellhole like their own. Have you seen their people?"

"Nope," Kacy said.

"No," Haze said. Could it be the Seekers that the Sister-hood had warned about?

"Consider yourself lucky," Camryn snapped and stormed off to the left of the path.

"Can you tell she was born here?" Kacy asked and veered to the right of the path.

The wave of people turned into a trickle as Haze followed Kacy back to the bunkhouse.

"Can I keep Hugh with us tonight?" she asked. It wasn't the best time to leave with these strange people stationed outside the wall. Haze wasn't sure that Kacy heard her and said, "Do you think I can—"

"If you leave, you're not going to find much out there. I'm surprised you didn't see that the first time," Kacy said as the bunkhouse and the sloped area that it sat on came into sight. "That's why I came back. Probably should've never left."

"What did you find out there?"

"Nothing but hard times. I spent most of my time trying to find food every day and dodging those men—if you want to call them that—who were looking for a girl like me. Some-one out there alone. I had no one, Haze."

Haze carefully said, "I've heard of groups of women that've banded together. Kind of like here."

Hugh looked up at her as they passed a row of glowing lanterns on the path. She squeezed his hand, and he snatched it away from her.

"Probably would've joined them if I'd found them. Probably wouldn't have stayed long. I want a family one day," she paused. "I just don't want to die to have one. So many women here have bad births."

"Haze! This isn't where I sleep," Hugh said, wrinkling his nose. Once again, he dragged his feet. "This place looks girly."

Inside the bunkhouse, the other women had returned. Haze guided Hugh over to her area. So this place housed the women that weren't members.

"I want to go back to my room with the other boys," Hugh said, folding his arms across his chest.

"No. I don't know where that is," Haze said, scanning the floor. Her knapsack remained half-hidden under the bed. "We can go there in the morning."

Hugh finally sat on her bed, but only a little. One of the women let out a loud sigh.

Kacy said, "Haze, have you met Fran and Irma?"

Fran sighed again and eyeballed Hugh. "Don't you think you should take him back to stay with the boys?"

"Someone go find Iris," Irma said with a laugh. "Or let him sleep outside."

Iris breezed into the room, almost as if Irma had summoned her. "I came to check on all of you and make sure you didn't need anything."

Hugh jumped to his feet and said, "I want to go back with the other boys."

"And that's exactly where you're going," Iris said, leaning over to look Hugh in the eye. "You have eyes just like your sisters."

Haze shook her head. There was a strange fire and possible attack. It was already late, and she was tired. Yet Iris was still on a ten with her energy. And she didn't believe for one second that Iris came for the other women.

No, Iris came to check on her. Haze lay back hard against the pillows as Hugh streaked for the door.

"Haze, I heard you were enjoying yourself at our celebration tonight," Iris said, and remained by the door.

And who told you that Haze wanted to ask. Kacy had already undressed and curled up under her covers.

Iris continued, "Lily and Amie told me you did a wonderful job this afternoon. And minding children is a job."

"Right," Haze said. She had babysat other children before she knew what she was doing or that there was a name for it.

"Well, have a good night," Iris said. She turned to leave and then stopped as if something had just occurred to her. "I almost forgot. The council wants to see you again tomorrow. We'll go there before you head to Lily's."

The silence in the room dropped like a cinderblock. Kacy's eyes briefly popped open, and she closed them again and pulled the covers over her head.

Chapter 10

Iris returned that morning with a small bundle of garments tucked under her arm. Once again, Haze dressed in clothes chosen by Iris to meet with Wes, Clint, and Myles. But this time, Iris gave her pants to wear, which Haze gleefully put on. When she stepped outside, the temperature felt much colder than the day before.

Haze tugged the jacket closed and wondered about what her mom was doing. Was Jess finding water for them? Was her aunt checking the traps every day so they would have food? Did her grandmother recover from her illness?

Iris's chatter from yesterday echoed in Haze's head. Life only got worse with the cold season almost upon them. That was why the Freemen opened up right before the cold season started. A lot of stray people died around this time. No one found their bodies until spring. But that was yesterday. Today, Iris hadn't said much.

"Did they find out who set that blaze?" Haze asked, touching her eye for a moment. For the first time since before she left the Sisterhood, she didn't have the edge of her sight blocked by that skin. It was still there, but not as much.

"Oh honey, I'm just not in the mood to talk about such a depressing event. But the good news is that we're still safe. And I can see both of your beautiful eyes."

Exactly when she needed more information, Iris was moody. They trekked to the other side of the community in silence. Haze noted the looping paths and the carefully sculpted bushes, hoping she could retrace the steps when the time came.

Inside the Sanctuary, it was quieter than the day before. A small fire crackled inside the massive fireplace and the men clustered in opposite corners in deep discussion.

Every man had a gun in his waistband.

The Sisterhood had cast them out without weapons except for some knives. Haze tried not to look obvious as she looked around for something, anything to defend herself.

She slowed up and let Iris continue and filched a palm-sized screwdriver from the windowsill.

Wes, Clint, and Myles had their backs to them while they stood in front of one of the giant windows.

Like the bunkhouses, the Sanctuary was on a slight hill, so the men had a view of the land, including the east wall, which now had soot stains.

Clint said, "I don't care what we have to do. We need to take them down. I know they set those fires somehow. We used a lot of our water to put it out. We're already short on it."

"We saw no one. I've had the guards questioned many times," Myles said.

"Hal was at the celebration, and even if he wasn't, he would've had too much drink in him anyway to spot anyone," Wes said.

Iris cleared her throat and the men turned around. Clint smiled even deeper than Wes at the sight of Haze and Iris. Myles also smiled. It reminded Haze of an animal baring its teeth.

Wes said, "Lily spoke to my wife yesterday, and she's raving about you. I have six headstrong boys. So, my wife can't wait to meet you." He pulled out a chair for Haze to sit down.

Haze nodded and stuffed her hands into her pockets, fighting the urge to pop her knuckles. All night she had tossed and turned, wondering why they wanted to meet with her again. Surely, it wasn't to praise her for skills at shepherding children.

Wes sat in the chair when Haze didn't move. Clint followed, dragging out the next chair. He drummed his fingers against the table as if Haze wasn't there. Myles's eyes probed her and made her shrink in her jacket.

She wasn't a member under their protection of women and children.

Familiar footsteps, light and quick, slapped against the wooden floors.

"Haze," Hugh shouted, and Ty followed and quickly poked him in the shoulder. Seconds later, Hugh whispered her name, "Haze."

Hugh snaked his arms around her and squeezed hard, almost lifting her from her feet. Haze lightly struggled and used the opportunity to turn her back to the men. The snuck a peek at Ty, who nodded to the three men.

"Your brother's strong for such a little guy," Wes said. "He's been trying to best my sons."

"And he's fast. He outran me to the breakfast table this morning, " Clint added.

"Did he?" Haze asked, with her back still to them. She stopped hugging Hugh and quickly looked into his eyes — *Hugh, you'd better not.*

"Hugh says that you were in the woods with your mom for a long time," Clint said.

Haze felt her knees tremble and her legs grow weak. Ty watched silently from the door. Haze didn't know what to say. How much had Hugh told them?

A tremor passed through Haze's ankles. She locked her knees before the shaking started there too.

Ty watched silently from the door.

Myles navigated around the table until he faced Haze. "I told them yesterday. You can't handle yourself. He turned his back to her and faced Wes and Clint. "She has hidden things from us. Yet, she wants to join us? How do we know she's not an invader? Here to trick us? Or," and his voice dropped to a cold whisper, "one of those strange girls raised by groups of women."

Haze turned to face them and Hugh turned as well, keeping his back to Haze. She crossed her arms around Hugh's shoulder as if protecting him, which kept her hands from trembling. And leaned on him heavily to hide her now weak knees. "I don't know any of those people," she said.

"Did you know about the fire? We never had this happen before until you showed up," the bowlegged holy man said, inching towards her.

"I don't know anything about that either," Haze said, and didn't know whether to back up or run. She hadn't done anything, and if he were a true seer, he would know that.

Why was this man so against her? If her grandmother were here, she would know.

"You're a seer. What do see?" Myles asked, sweeping his arm out as if he expected Haze to put on a show. "Tell us."

"Nothing. I don't see—" Haze said, right before something fluttered at the edge of her memory. The vision of the man dying in the field came back to her. "I don't know anything about the fires."

"Ty?" Wes asked. "Was she at the celebration with you? The whole time?"

"I picked her up from Lily's," Ty said, quietly.

Haze held her breath. She had only left him a few moments.

Ty continued," I was with her throughout."

"Haze doesn't make any fires unless we need to cook," Hugh said, and squeezed

Haze's hand. "All Haze does is help everybody. That's what my grandmom said."

"Hugh," Haze said, silently begging him to be quiet.

"Your grandma? Where is she? Was she with you in the woods?" Clint asked.

"She's dead," Hugh said and then pressed his face into Haze's side.

"Can I have some water?" Haze asked, wishing she had sat when she had the chance. She dabbed at the sweat prickling against her face and neck.

"The water is for our citizens," Clint said, nodding at Iris. "But we can spare an extra cup for today. Only for you."

Wes seemed to check the expressions of Clint and Myles and said, "Myles is our seer and he sees something in you. So if you're not a seer, why do you have that veil over your eye?"

"Precisely my question," Myles said.

"Veil? I told you something bit me," Haze replied, squinting at Myles for just a moment before lowering her gaze to the top of Hugh's head. Myles had to be older than her mother, despite the lack of gray hair or any hair on his dome-head. "But since you're a seer, shouldn't you have seen that fire coming?"

Ty coughed and pounded his chest. But not before Haze caught a slight stifled laugh.

Myles cut a swift look in Ty's direction. "This girl from the Deadwoods, who has no family and no home, thinks this is a game," he said, folding himself with ease into the chair between Clint and Wes. "Tell me something. Tell me, tell us what will happen in the next few days here? If you can't answer this as a seer, then what good are you? You'll allow us to be destroyed."

With her arms still resting on Hugh's shoulders, Hugh caught hold of her hands under his chin and squeezed them.

Iris returned with a small cup of water. Haze drank most of it in one swallow. The rest spilled down her chin. Iris took the cup from her.

Myles leaned back in his chair and asked, "What have you seen, girl? Tell us."

"Visitors are coming," Haze said, struggling with the words.

Myles threw his head back, and his laughter ricocheted around the room.

"We've already had visitors. Last night, remember?" Clint said wryly, tilting back in his chair. "Last week, it was you and your brother."

"Not that kind. It'll be more than two but less than five. And they're not strangers," Haze said, with as much confidence as she could dreg up in the presence of these men.

"When?" Wes asked.

"Within six days," she replied.

"You expect us to believe that?" Myles asked.

"I gave you what you asked," she replied, although she wasn't sure how or if it was true. The Sisterhood had taught her that Seekers often moved in pairs. So there had to be more than one person setting the fire. But not more than three or four or it would attract attention.

Wes stopped drumming his fingers. "If no one shows up in six days, you and your brother will be returned to the Deadwoods," he said.

"No. No, Haze," Hugh said, tugging at Haze's arms. "I don't want to go."

Haze sucked in her breath. So Hugh's allegiance had already shifted.

"I think Lily's waiting on her," Iris said, and the three men left the table and returned to the window as if Haze had disappeared.

When Haze turned to leave, Ty was already gone.

CHAPTER 11

Lily escorted Haze to the back of the cavernous home she shared with Clint, which had multiple bedrooms and a private deck centered outside their bedroom.

"Where's Amie?" Haze asked.

"She lives in the opposite end of the house."

"Your dwelling is so large," she said, standing over the large circular tub built into the floor. Steam rose from the water. Did her grandmother use something like this when she was a young woman?

"My what?" Lily asked.

"Your house."

"What a peculiar word for a house," Lily said. What shelter did you have in the Deadwoods?"

"Nothing much. Just whatever we found that other people had left," Haze said and took a sip of the second cup of water that she'd had since she'd been there that morning.

All the children were outside playing, and Haze had spent the morning picking up their clothes. And then plucking the feathers from three chickens to prepare enough food for Clint, Lily, Amie, and children for that evening.

Haze checked the small firepit built near the back entrance. It was big enough to hold this big pot of stew.

Haze had wandered by enough houses near her bunkhouse to know that they didn't have firepits. And they didn't have water barrels either. She barely had anything to drink at the bunkhouse. Kacy had told her that each home received a weekly ration of water.

"You're lucky to be here," Lily said.

"That's what everyone tells me," Haze replied, chopping up a stack of carrots and sliding them by the already chopped mound of onions. When Lily had her back turned, Haze quickly ate some of the carrot slices.

"You don't believe that?" Lily asked and shook out the huge pot, her whole body jiggling as she did.

"I'm still getting used to it," Haze said. She had already shaken out the pot and made sure no critters were hiding in it before they put food in it.

"You better get used to it quick. You'll be doing this for yourself soon enough."

"Cooking?"

"Keeping house for your family. We marry at 16 here. I know it wasn't like that before, but since the Destruction, that's what we do."

Haze filched a small knife from the drawer and hid that in her jacket. She had never thought of marrying. Her grandmother's and mother's stories of marriage were for the pre-Destruction women.

The Sisterhood had formed families, but marriage wasn't discussed.

Haze wrapped three carrots in cloth and stuck them inside her jacket pocket, along with two potatoes.

"In a society like this, you'll have your pick," she put the pot down, turned it over, and sat on it.

"Were you born here?"

Lily laughed and said, "Not at all. I was brought here by my aunt when I was ten or eleven. I'd mostly lived in the woods with her. Not the Deadwoods, though. My mom died giving birth to me, so my aunt raised me. Things were so hard all the time. And the men—the men there — were the worst."

"I didn't see many in the Deadwoods," Haze said. Not this time, but she did before they went into the Sisterhood after her father had left. In fact, that was the reason they searched for the Sisterhood or any community. Haze had been in the woods with Jess picking mushrooms. Jess had went near one tree in particular that had the oyster shaped mushrooms blooming out of the tree itself. Haze saw the shadow of someone against the tree and told Jess they needed to leave.

She and Jess returned to their shelter where Haze's mom was napping with her arms curled around her large belly. Haze didn't wake her but told her grandmother instead. Her grandmother returned to the area with her and checked but found no one.

But her grandmother insisted they leave the shelter, and they did. They traveled for two days but couldn't go for much longer. Haze overheard her mother saying she was spotting and afraid she'd lose the baby. They pitched their tents near a small cave.

That night, six men attacked. Haze, with her mother and Jess, crawled into the cave and hid, trying to block out her aunt and grandmother's screams of terror.

The next morning, her bloody and badly bruised grandmother had said, "We need somewhere with other people. Good people. I don't want my granddaughters hunted by these men like this."

But it took weeks for her grandmother and aunt to heal enough to walk. Haze couldn't remember how soon after they found the Sisterhood. But even then, her aunt didn't speak much after that.

"Are you feeling well? Your eyes are all glassy," Lily asked, and Haze jumped, not realizing the woman stood beside her. "Well, girl, I didn't mean to scare you like that. Don't do that to me. I'm liable to drop this baby right here on the floor."

"As long as you're squatting when you do it," Haze said, shaking off the memories. But not the fear that her family might face that attack again. And her grandmother was much older now, and she no longer had her guns. Someone in the Sisterhood stole them. They never found out who did it.

"Squatting?" Lily asked and shuddered. "I've never heard of such a thing. It might hurt my baby. I can't lose another one."

"How many have you lost?"

"Three boys. Two had the cords wrapped around their necks. And the last one," she sighed and returned to sitting on the pot. "He was a breech, and I lost so much blood I thought I was going to die with her. I almost did. Clint's other wives have had bad births too. So many of the women here die trying to give life."

"How many midwives do you have?" Haze asked. She'd never heard of a woman dying in childbirth. Pregnant woman had turned up at the Sisterhood and never had a problem giving birth.

"How many what?"

"Midwives. To help you with the baby before you give birth. I used to help my grandmother do it," Haze said before she could stop herself.

As she said it, a vision unfolded in front of her. Clint and Lily with a baby wrapped in a sheet and lowering it into the ground. And Amie was there with Wes, his wives, and their children. Myles was also there with his wife. No children were with them.

A light came on in Lily's eyes, and she said, "Did you?" She rubbed her belly, thoughtfully.

"I didn't do much," Haze said.

Lily asked, "Can you check on the children? I don't hear them as much and that makes me nervous."

"That will take longer than chopping these carrots," Haze replied.

Once outside, Haze went in the direction of the children that led to a small fenced off area. But Haze continued past it. She didn't run so that she wouldn't draw attention to herself.

But she headed towards the south gate, which wasn't in the view of the Sanctuary and also wasn't the one that Hal guarded. She said a silent goodbye to Hugh and hoped he'd grow up to be one of the good men. Not like her father or the men in the Deadwoods.

She surveyed behind her and saw no one and sped up her pace. It was still early, and she could escape before sundown. The only thing was that on each side of the community were fields before you reached the gate. That way, the men in the towers saw anyone coming to the gate inside the community and outside of it.

Instead of going through the field, she doubled back to the path to circle around it. It would take much longer. Still, it was the better choice. The gray skies darkened in the distance. There was some sort of storm happening miles away. Either it was headed for this area, or she would run into it. That might keep anyone off her trail. Wait, who said the Freemen would search for her, anyway?

On the road ahead, three boys approached, and they appeared to be about her age. And also were like steps in height. The shortest boy had small eyes, which reminded Haze of a lizard. They slowed as she got closer, and Haze's stomach clenched. She was alone. But wait, this was the Freemen community. Still —

"That's her," the short boy said to the two other boys.

Haze continued past them and also gently shook her head so that her bang slipped over her eyes, shading them.

"Hey," the second boy said, and he was the stockiest of the three boys. Not quite Ty's height, but almost there. He jumped in front of her and leaned in close, much like Myles had done. "Aren't you that new girl?

"Nope," she tried to go around him.

"Get out of her way, Walker," the third boy said. "Let her pass."

"Shut up, Reed," Walker said and blocked her path. "I saw you last night at the celebration. With your brother?"

"I don't know who you saw, but I had a sister, and she died giving birth last quarter. Everyone knows that."

That silenced them.

"Told you it wasn't her. Nothing's wrong with her eyes," Reed said, ribbing his short friend with his elbow.

Haze caught her breath. How many people here knew about her eye? No one in her family had ever said much about it. But here it meant something. Probably because of Myles.

They finally let her pass.

"Don't you know the gate's closed that way?" Walker shouted after her. "They won't let you out without a pass."

Haze kept going. But she thought she heard one of the boy's say, "I still think that's her."

The sun had changed positions before Haze closed in on the gate. There was no way she could bypass any of the guards. The cinderblock walls rose up about 20 feet and had this strange wire strung through spikes implanted at the top of the wall. Rows of shrubs lined the interior of the wall, no doubt laced with traps.

Ten to twelve guards, including one woman guard, encircled two strange women. The clothes on the women hung like rags and one carried a baby in her arms.

Haze drew as close as she dared.

The woman holding the baby said, "Please let us stay. We have no family and no one to help us."

The second woman said, "We can work. I know how to grow food."

The guards seemed unmoved by their pleas. What happened to the week that allowed people to join?

Haze eased closer.

The woman guard said, "Listen, we let you in last year, and you didn't follow the rules."

"We didn't know the rules," said their male companion. Haze hadn't noticed him. She had already grown accustomed to all males being from this society. He wore almost the same rags as the women. What had happened to these people? Her family never looked like that no matter how long they had lived in the woods.

"Yes, you did. You didn't care," the guard said. We'll give you some provisions for your troubles. You can stay here for the night. But you have to leave in the morning."

One of the male guards on the outskirts of the group spotted Haze and tapped another guard on the shoulder. The guards wore gear just like Ty's gear. She realized that Ollie and Roy had different clothes than Ty.

Haze backed up as the guards approached her.

CHAPTER 12

The three strangers looked briefly in her direction and continued to plead with the unrelenting guards. The wind whipped with force across the wall and blew her hair back.

Haze blinked against the mist of rain.

Far off, the sky was no longer gray but almost black, and thunder forked through the sky.

The woman guard said, "Are you lost?"

"I was just out walking."

"Walking where?" the second guard asked and skimmed her up and down. "Just about every gal here knows to keep away from the gates unless they need something."

Like Ollie, Roy, and Hal, he was an older guard with a hard, round belly that hung over his pants. They rationed the water and food here. Where did that belly come from?

"I'm done with it," Haze said and turned to leave.

The male guard grabbed her by the arm. "Hold it," he said. "Aren't you that girl that was just brought in here?"

Haze guessed that the Freemen had about 700 or 800 people here. Was it only her eye that made her stand out?

"That's me. I guess I did get lost," she said, and the feeling that she'd had early with Clint, Wes, and especially Myles returned. "I was just seeing how big this place was. Everyone says that there's a lot to explore."

The female guard eyed her, and her eyes held no hint of compassion as she said, "I expect you're supposed to help the families. That's the reason you're allowed to stay. If you can't contribute, then you can leave like those parasites." She nodded in the direction of the three people.

"I'm going now," Haze said, finally pulling her arm from the guard's vice grip. She turned so quickly that she nearly tripped over her feet.

Both guards caught her before she hit the ground. She saw the woman guard quickly zeroed-in on her left eye.

The male guard zeroed-in on everything besides her eye.

Haze pulled away from them and took her time, heading down the path until she was out of their sight.

Then Haze ran and returned to the fenced-off area and all of Lily and Amie's children were gone. She bent over double to catch her breath.

What now?

She could return to the bunkhouse or go to Lily's door.

Haze retraced her steps from earlier that morning and, using the sun as a guide, headed back to the east side of the community.

***

Haze returned to the bunkhouse yet hadn't seen Iris all afternoon. She fully expected the woman to bust through the door with a smile and some scented water spray.

It never happened.

Gradually, Irma, and Fran arrived around sunset, and both appeared weary. Both women wore overalls covered in dirt, which they promptly took off.

"You're here already?" Fran asked. "I'da thought Clint would keep you tied down with his brood until well after dinner."

"No, I got to leave early," Haze said, opening her coat and keeping her back to them. She quickly placed the stolen food in her basket. "So, where are you both from? Did you come here together?"

"Not at all," Fran replied. "I was part of another community for a long time. Since the—what do they call it here—the Destruction? It didn't have a lot of people. There were maybe 50 of us. Most of the people there were older than me and they started dying. I wasn't about to be left out there alone. So here I am. I'd heard about this group some time ago and almost joined them years ago. But changed my mind. I had a husband at the time, so there was no real need."

"What about you, Irma? Did you live in another community before the Freemen?" Haze asked and waited for Irma to say something, but the woman didn't and kept her back to Haze while undressing.

But not before Haze glimpsed the lightning-shaped marks across her belly. So Irma had kids somewhere.

"I know they brought you here," Fran said in a breezy tone, "but what made them go after you? I've never heard of them doing that."

"I don't know," Haze replied. She hadn't told anyone how they brought her in. It was bad enough that they talked about her eye. What else was next?

"Did you sneak up on them and steal from them?" Irma asked. "I'm not saying that you did. I'm just asking."

"I didn't know they were there," Haze said, carefully measuring her words. These women were old enough to be her mother or aunts. Like Iris, their smiles didn't reach their eyes whenever they smiled, which didn't seem often. What had she done to them to make them so cold? "But it was me and my brother and they didn't want to see us left out there alone."

"You'll have a ring on your finger before long," Fran said, and for the first time a true smile lit up her eyes. "But I'll have mine first."

"If she wants a ring," Irma said, suspiciously.

The door opened and Iris came inside, leading the two women that Haze had seen earlier near the gate.

The women no longer wore rags, and the baby wasn't with them either.

"We have two empty beds right here," Iris said, and pointed to the corner beds right next to Haze.

But Iris didn't acknowledge Haze at all. So, did she know what Haze had done?

Iris continued, "Ladies, this is Trena and Bailey. They'll be here for tonight only."

Trena and Bailey went to the corner beds with their mouths poked out. Trena rolled her eyes at Haze and turned her back with an exaggerated jerk.

Haze scooted her knapsack fully under the bed.

Both women were bone thin.

Trena wore pants that swallowed her thin frame. And a dirty coat with no shirt underneath.

Bailey's stained jacket and dirty pants fit her better.

Iris said, "I'll be back in the morning. We'll take good care of your little one for the night."

"Whatever," Trena said, waving a thin arm as if to shoo Iris away. "Just feed him on time like I told you."

Fran snorted in disgust.

The moment that Iris closed the door, Trena, who was closest to Haze, flung one of the small washing cloths at Fran and said, "Aren't you too old to join?"

"And too ugly," Bailey said with a snicker, showing off the tooth missing on the side.

"Not as long as I'm healthy. So worry about yourself," Fran said with narrowed eyes.

Irma added, "The Freemen don't just accept—anybody—here. You and your friend look like you've been in the Deadwoods a long time."

"Long enough to know how to survive it," Bailey said with a hard stare. The woman took in every inch of the room as if committing it to memory. "We're here now. With you."

"We'll see," Fran said.

Trena flicked a glance at Haze. "Can I swap beds with you? I don't like corners."

"I don't like them either," Haze said, and since she was already sitting on the bed, she kicked back against the pillow. They could have it once she left.

Bailey turned her hard stare in Haze's direction. "Didn't I see you earlier? What were those guards asking you about?" she asked.

Both Fran and Irma quickly sat on their beds as if it was story time.

"Nothing. They knew I was just seeing what's here," Haze said, wishing the woman would shut up.

Trena was about the same height as Haze and that's where the similarity ended. She was probably around Ty's age, but she looked older. And her mouth stayed twisted into an angry scowl.

"So, they're letting you stay?" Trena asked.

"That's a dumb question," Fran said. "Look at her."

"I got the feeling that I've seen you somewhere before," Trena said. "Like you were part of some other group."

"I saw you by the gate too," Haze said, quickly rising. "Anyone seen Kacy? I haven't seen her today?"

When no one answered, Haze made a beeline for the outside. She had seen Trena before today too. When Phoenyx had turned her and Kyle and Bailey away from the Sisterhood. And Trena looked just as mean and angry as before. So when Haze spotted their shelter after her family was put out of the Sisterhood, she knew to stay away from them.

Yet, here Trena was again with Kyle and the other woman. Why did they stay with Kyle if they had to beg for shelter?

Ty ran up the road towards her.

"Oh no," she muttered. Something was wrong and Haze ran to meet him.

CHAPTER 13

Like in her bunkhouse, candles lit the windows of the homes against the freezing night air. And a half moon hung in the sky, just as it had the last night she'd seen her family.

The lanterns on the ground shook as Haze pounded past them. Nothing moved in the shadows. She didn't have to keep watch at night here.

Ty came to a stop in the grass before Haze. Haze tried to stop as well, but her momentum carried her forward another foot so that she rammed into him.

Ty didn't budge, but Haze lost her footing. Grabbing her by the arms, Ty caught her before she hit the cold ground.

Haze struggled to get her feet underneath herself and untangle from him. "Is Hugh okay?" she asked.

"He's fine. It's Amie. She needs your help."

"Ty wait," Haze said, dragging her feet just as Hugh had done to her. "I don't want any trouble. Myles doesn't want me here."

"But Clint does. Amie's in labor. I'll stay with you and make sure nothing happens."

Haze relaxed just a little. "Lily should be due first," she said, and Ty shrugged.

Haze followed Ty, noting the twists and turns in the path while trying to remember the few times she'd helped her grandmother deliver a baby or had half-listened to her giving the mom-to-be belly massages and advice.

When they arrived at Clint's home, the lanterns silhouetted the father-to-be pacing back and forth.

"Listen, I heard that you bailed on them today. Don't say anything if they bring it up," Ty said, stomping the fresh mud from his boots. Even though it hadn't rained enough over the Freemen community for mud. "I have something to ask you when you're done."

Clint opened the door and beckoned them inside.

Ty nudged Haze in front of him.

Amie's groans climbed the walls and made goosebumps creep along Haze's arms. She'd heard birthing sounds before, but not like that.

Haze quickly pushed Clint aside and followed the noise.

Two men and a woman had Amie propped up on a table covered with fluid-soaked sheets. Each man held one of Amie's arms. Amie twisted and turned and thrashed like a wild and wounded animal. She bit down on the piece of cloth in her mouth, muffling her shrieks.

Lily was nowhere to be found.

"What are you doing to her?" Haze asked, pushing against the first man. He didn't move but held onto Amie's arm as if it belonged to him. "Amie is giving birth. She's not a dog in heat for you to restrain."

The slow fire of anger flickered in the first man's eyes.

"It's too soon. Amie wasn't due yet," Clint said, and anguish filled his voice, unlike the calm voice Haze had heard from him the past few days. "It's another breech. He might have the cord wrapped around his neck again."

"He?" Haze asked.

"Myles predicted it'd be a boy," the first man said.

"It's a girl. She's been carrying high," Haze replied, taking a clean cloth and patting Amie's sweaty forehead.

The two men and Clint exchanged glances.

Another groan from Amie swallowed the silence. She twisted again on the table, trying to find a comfortable position.

"The first man said, "Look, we're like the doctors here. We've delivered many of the kids here. My father was a real doctor before the Destruction."

Haze's good eye twitched, and she said, "I have to wash up. When I return, you and him need to let go of her so she can get off that table and get on all fours. Put another blanket on the floor. Clint, you have a large bathing tub. Fill it with warm water."

Her grandmother had told long stories about some of the doctors from her day, male and female. There were good ones who had deep knowledge and sought the best for their patients.

And then there was the rest of them.

She'd have to ask Kacy if these men were responsible for delivering her newborn niece. So that the mother and newborn died in the process.

Once Haze made the two men leave and put Amie in a squatting position, it didn't take long to deliver the small baby girl with no cord wrapped around her neck.

By that time, the sun broke through the horizon. Haze returned to the water barrel to wash up again and hoped that she could go back to the bunkhouse and sleep.

Lily hovered by the water barrel, getting herself a cup, and said, "Amie's not half as torn up as the last time. We already have some of those herbs you told her about.:

"It'll help her heal quickly," Haze replied uneasily.

"You certainly learned a lot from your grandmother. We don't have any midwives here."

And you still don't Haze wanted to say. Instead, she said, "She was a very wise woman."

"Was? So she's dead?"

Haze hesitated. Had Hugh said something different the other morning? "I don't know. She was sick the last time I saw her."

"Before you came here? I heard you were by the gate this afternoon and not at the park with the children. Do you really want to be out there sick and doing everything for yourself by yourself? Do you really believe you can do better alone?"

"I believe I'm able to make my own choice just like my grandmother did, and my mother," Haze said.

"You better make the right one. Nothing good will happen for you if you don't. Then you'll come back three years from now begging to join. Like Kacy. Or worse, the ones that are lodging with you in the visitor's quarters," Lily said and handed Haze a bowl of water. "Wait here. I've sent for Ty to take you back to the bunkhouse."

But Haze put more small potatoes in her pockets and slipped away while Clint and Amie cooed over their new baby girl, Nyomi.

She didn't want Ty asking her any questions. It was his fault, along with Ollie and Roy, that she was here in the first place.

If they had left her alone, she'd be with her family right now. Instead of this place ruled by Freemen.

She returned as quietly as possible to the bunkhouse and in the rising sunlight drifted past the outlines of Fran, Irma, and Kacy in their beds.

And the outline of someone in her bed.

Haze sighed.

Trena was a problem. No wonder they wanted to get rid of her.

Haze pulled back the covers to tell the woman to get in her own bed.

But it wasn't just Trena in her bed. It was also the man that had been with Trena and Bailey earlier that day. And neither he nor Trena had a stitch of clothing on.

The man opened his eyes, and a slow smile spread across his lips. "Back already?"

Chapter 14

A rush of wind knocked against the side of the bunkhouse, which made Haze jump. The man's smirk deepened. He had pushed Trena and Haze's bed together, so he'd have a bigger bed. Bailey still slept in the bed assigned to her.

They'd left Haze nowhere to sleep. If she went for Iris then Myles would hear of it. She wished that she'd waited for Ty. He would handle this man right now.

Haze picked up the small bowl by her bed, and it was empty of water. The man continued to watch her while Trena snored.

This was what the Sisterhood had warned about. The men here watched her, too. But in the bunkhouse, she wanted to sleep in peace away from the prying eyes of the men and the women.

If her mother were here, she'd tell Haze to handle it.

"Stop looking at me," Haze said, sending the tin bowl flying towards his head, and he batted it away.

The bowl bounced off the wall and landed on Kacy, who woke up.

"What's going on?" Kacy asked, rolling over and rubbing one eye. That one eye opened wide when she saw the couple in the bed next to her. "He can't be in here."

Trena stretched and said, "Calm down, girl. Kyle ain't going to hurt you."

"I have nowhere to sleep," Haze said.

"You wasn't here," Trena said, dragging the covers up over the both of them.

"He needs to leave," Haze said.

"Says who?" Trena said.

"Us," Kacy said.

"We got a bunch of scared little girls in here," Trena said, and she and Kyle laughed.

Irma kicked off her blanket, and her feet hit the floor with a thump. "Well, let me go get the guards, and we'll see who gets the last laugh around here. Haze, you can sleep here," she said.

Trena and Kyle stopped laughing, and he quickly reached for his clothes.

Irma pulled on a jacket and disappeared out the door.

Haze had barely taken off her jacket and sat on Irma's bed when the woman returned. And with her were three burly men from the bunkhouse across the path.

Kyle had fully dressed by that time, along with Trena and Bailey.

Bailey glared at Haze and said, "I can't believe I have to get up for this. How old are you?"

The three men entered and quickly filled the tiny space.

"You're threatening these women and girls?" the first man asked. A river of veins protruded from his uncovered arms.

"My brother didn't do nothing," Bailey said.

"They were in my bed with no clothes on," Haze said, still sitting on Irma's bed. She folded a leg under her and swung the other foot off the bed. "I call that something."

Kyle said, "I wasn't—"

The first man grabbed Kyle by the collar and jerked him out the door. Trena and Bailey's screams pierced the morning air. Kacy clapped her hand over her mouth, and Haze clapped hers over her ears at the sound of Kyle's body slamming against the bunkhouse over and over.

Trena and Bailey's screams reminded her of her grandmother and aunt's screams from long ago.

"I guess I can't count on getting more sleep," Fran said.

Irma curled back under the covers and pulled them over her head.

***

Haze woke up to Iris spraying her with something scented.

Iris sat on the bed across from her in the almost empty bunkhouse and said, "I heard that you had an exciting night and morning."

When Haze turned over, Ty stood at the foot of her bed with his arms folded behind his back. Did men ever smile? Haze couldn't remember if her father had smiled much.

"It's already midday," Iris said, and just like yesterday, she painted on a hesitant smile.

"You need to come with us," Ty said.

Haze tried to read him, if he was upset that she hadn't waited for him the night before. But Ty appeared no different from each time she'd seen him. She took a deep breath and asked, "Is the baby all right? Is Amie?"

"Get dressed and meet us outside," Iris said, rising from the bed and following Ty, who had already turned on his heel and left.

Chapter 15

Haze didn't keep them waiting long. Once outside, she jerked her hand from the wooden handle on the bunkhouse door. It, along with door, had a splattering of hastily wiped blood on it from when Kyle hit it earlier. She shook her hand as if she had scalded it.

Ty and Iris stood side-by-side, watching her.

"I'll make sure that's cleaned properly," Iris said with a hesitant smile.

Haze silently rehearsed her reason for leaving Amie and Clint without waiting for Ty. But it didn't matter because her knapsack was ready to go. Today, she'd get Hugh and disappear back into the woods.

"We had a situation at the gate this morning," Ty said, and he switched positions so that Haze remained in the center with Iris on the other side of her. "Two women asked to be let in. The oldest said she had her granddaughter in here. She described you, Haze. Didn't your brother say your grandmother was dead?"

"He was scared. Myles scared him," Haze said and stumbled over her own foot at the sharp turn of Iris's head in her direction. The last thing she needed was anyone telling Myles that she was talking about him. "I mean, you all scared him. He's only seven."

"He told me he was five," Ty said.

"He doesn't know how to count," Haze said quickly. She grabbed ahold of Ty's arm, and he paused. "But what happened to those women? Where are they? Did you let them in?"

Iris pried Haze's fingers from Ty's arm. "We're holding them at the gate," she said, shooting a dark look at Ty.

Haze whooped with joy.

"No, they're still outside the gate," Ty said, and thoughtfully rubbed the spot on his arm where her fingers had gripped.

They crossed two fields and arrived at the same gate entrance that Haze had used three days earlier. As usual, the men with their weapons patrolled the area.

Ty said, "Hal, we're taking Haze through. Let her see these others."

Haze went through gates with Hal's gun trained on her back.

Outside the gate, about fifty feet away, her grandmother lay on the ground wrapped in a blanket, and Haze's mother sat next to her. The wind whipped against their cloth sacks and other belongings strewn around them.

"Sister-grandmother," Haze screamed and kicked up the dust running to her.

Haze slid to a stop and kneeled. Her grandmother opened her eyes, which were clouded with sadness and fear.

"There you are," she said and reached up and patted Haze's cheek before closing her eyes again.

Her grandmother seemed like she'd aged years in just a few weeks. Haze stroked her grandmother's soft gray hair, which curled like a pepper plant after a heavy rain, and leaned over to hug her mother.

Haze squeezed them both so tight she was sure she'd snap their bones. "Where's Jess? And Sister-aunt?" she asked.

"They stayed behind. Jess told us what happened," Haze's mother said, returning the fierce hug. "She told us what those men did."

"Was Jess...hurt?"

"No. But, let me look at you," she cupped Haze's face with both hands. "Did they hurt you? Have they done *anything* to you?"

Haze, almost against her will, skimmed over her shoulder at Ty, still by the gate with Hal and the other guards. "No, they haven't hurt me. I haven't had to search for water one time. And I have my own bed. I get it in each night with a full stomach."

"I could use that too," her grandmother said in a voice barely above a whisper.

"Sister-grandmother needs water. She's still ill. She can't go any further like this," her mother said.

Haze rose and returned to the gate. "My grandmother's sick. She needs to come inside. She needs help," she said.

"Not until our leaders say so. Those are the Freemen's rules," Hal said, tapping his weapon as if he had forgotten it was there. "I don't make them."

"Hal, please. This is my family," Haze said, and almost seized him by the arm like she had done Ty minutes earlier. But the other guard's presence and their casual resting of their hands on their weapons stopped her. "Can I speak to Clint? Please let me speak to Clint. Ty, is Iris still waiting? Can't you get Clint?"

"They'll have to stay out here," Ty said, adding, "I'll tell them, but they may not come right away."

"No, just tell Clint, not Myles."

"It doesn't work that way," he said, and then held up his hand before she spoke again. "I'm going to them now."

Ty removed a small pouch from around his belt and handed it to her.

Haze squeezed the liquid filled pouch and ran back to her grandmother. She pulled the cork out and lifted her grandmother's head and helped her drink a few swallows. After a few moments, her mother snatched it and the women took turns until they'd drained it.

Haze's mother pushed the cork back into the top, her eyes roving Haze's clothes. "What's that you're wearing?"

"They gave it to me."

"Who are they?" Haze's mother asked.

"The Freemen."

"The Freemen? You were snatched by men calling themselves free men?" Haze's mother asked, her voice rising in disbelief.

Her grandmother opened her eyes and said weakly, "I've heard of them before. One of them at the Sisterhood told me."

"Just rest. You don't have to say anything," Haze said to her grandmother.

Hal paced at the gate for the rest of the afternoon. Haze went to him several times, but he wouldn't let them enter.

Finally, right before sunset, Iris arrived, and Hal escorted her out of the gate.

Where had Ty gone?

"Ladies," Iris said and hurried towards them, with her arms thrown open in a greeting, "I'm here to bring you inside. First, we need to check your things."

Relief rushed through Haze like an early morning tide, and she almost cried. Haze gathered their stuff while the guards helped her grandmother up. She'd never seen her grandmother this weak before.

The guards checked every item in their bags and Iris said, "Your things will have to stay here. We'll give you some new things inside."

None of the woman protested. They just nodded.

Iris continued, "We have visitor's quarters that aren't too far from this entrance. Let's get you over there. Haze has different quarters."

Haze opened her mouth to protest, but her grandmother launched into a coughing fit, which shook her body and almost made her knees buckle.

Hal and Iris steadied her.

Iris chattered away, as usual, while escorting them, and Haze was strangely comforted by that. Two guards accompanied them, and her grandmother leaned heavily on one while they carried her sacks.

One guard offered to take the sacks from the two women.

"I can carry my own things," Haze's mother replied. "I've done it for years."

Haze's mother had no issues walking, but she was much slower than before. What had happened to them in such a short time? Her mother stopped and handed one of her sacks to Haze, who strained under the weight but still took the sack.

Her mother hadn't had those shadows underneath her eyes when they left the Sisterhood, nor the hollowness to her voice.

This was the Freemen's fault. They'd terrorized her family.

The visitor's quarters were the same size as the bunkhouse, but the wood was a lighter color, unlike the hickory-colored bunkhouse. The quarters held six beds, and two appeared occupied already. The windows weren't as big, and unlike the bunkhouse, this place was out in the open with no other buildings or structures around it. Not even trees. The guard tower had a clear line of sight of whoever entered and exited the quarters.

Once inside the quarters, her grandmother immediately got into the nearest bed. Haze set down the sacks with a loud thump. Her shoulders ached from the short travel.

Her mother looked around and asked, "Haze, where's Hugh? Where's my little boy?" All exhaustion seemed to leave her in an instant. Panic crept into her voice. She refused to sit down or put her things down and turned to Iris, "Where's my son?"

"He's fine," Iris said. "He's housed with the other boys. Probably just finished helping them build a new table or something."

"I want to see him."

"We'll bring him to you," Iris said.

"Right now."

"I'll have to get him. It might take a bit of time. There's a lot of land in here."

"Mom, Hugh's fine," Haze said, wrapping her in another hug before turning to Iris. "My grandmother needs some food and medicine."

"Ty's getting some supplies and sent me ahead. He knew this was your family," Iris replied.

"Iris, thank you."

"Don't thank me, thank Ty. He's the one that believed them. Hal was ready to send them away."

"Ty has an eye for the truth," Haze replied.

"And I have a nose for lying," Iris said and motioned for Haze to follow. Once they were outside the door, she said in a low voice, "Our open membership ended yesterday. Your family can stay through the morning, but they have to leave after that. And Wes, Myles, and Clint have said that you can leave with them."

Chapter 16

In the bunkhouse, the women milled around, still in their work clothes, and had already heard about the arrival of Haze's family by the time Haze returned. Irma and Fran had helped out in the fields along with Kacy. And now they removed them and washed up. If Haze closed her eyes, it was almost like being back in the Sisterhood. Almost.

Irma said, "I got me a personal invitation to the next celebration. I'm going with Gus."

"When's that?" Haze asked. The last thing she needed was another distraction.

"Next week, so I heard," Fran replied. "And since your family's here, they can go too. So, now you won't be so anxious." She paused and studied Haze's face. "You really need to relax. That's the point of being here."

In bed, Haze tossed and turned half the night and listened to the wind howl while Irma, Fran, and Kacy slept peacefully. Why couldn't she be like these other women? Why couldn't she be like Kacy, who, despite her sister's death, continued with her plans?

She'd received no word from Ty or the Council.

The next morning, Iris showed up early and, to Haze's surprise, she had Haze's mother with her. "Come look inside," Haze said, guiding her into their quarters. "Sister-mother--" and then wanted to kick herself at the expressions on the women's faces. "Mom, this is Kacy, Fran, and Irma."

In an instant, Fran and Irma surveyed Haze's mother from head to foot.

"I see where she gets her beauty from," Irma said, and instead of putting on her overalls, she put on regular pants. "I don't have to work the field today with the fellas. I get to watch some kids for the morning. I guess your good fortune rubbed off on me, Haze."

Iris said to Haze's mother, "Haze has helped out the wives with their children. I don't think she'll be doing that today."

Her mother sat next to Haze on her bed. She still had shadows under her eyes. "I saw Hugh this morning," she said, "and he's already gaining weight. I can't believe how my little boy has grown in just a few weeks."

Haze hadn't seen any height difference in him. But with regular meals, he was healthier.

Her mother continued, "You should've seen him playing with those other boys." And she gave her first hint of a smile.

"That's why I liked…" Haze said and then checked over her shoulder. Iris waited by the door but still within hearing distance. She still needed to speak with Iris, who avoided her gaze. "I had the other girls to play with when I had time."

Kacy also put on overalls.

And Iris asked, "Do you have an extra pair? Give them to Haze? Make sure you tell them that she'll do Fran's work."

Kacy reached into the basket next to her bed and tossed them over to Haze.

"Why?" Haze asked and picked up the rough, blue gear. She'd never worn such a thing.

Haze's mother said, "That woman told me what you've been doing, and I told her that you like real work."

"Sounds like you'll be coming with me," Kacy said.

Kacy took her to the fields and explained what to do while Iris escorted her mother back to the visitor's quarters.

The damp earth perfumed the air before they reached the fields. Other teens and adults gathered the last crops in the fields.

After introducing Haze to Barney, the old man that co-ordinated all the people in the fields, Haze followed Kacy to a row of turnips and to her surprise, two of the nearby boys were the ones that she'd run into the day before while sneaking to the gate.

Kacy said, "This is Walker," and he was the one that had blocked her the second time, "and this is Reed," the one who hadn't believed her. On the other side of Reed, Haze recognized the girl from the celebration. Kacy added, "That's Camryn, the do-gooder."

"Not on your life," Camryn said, flinging a clump of dirt at Kacy. "Guess Fran's not coming. Good thing. She was getting on my nerves."

"Mine too," Walker said. "These old people don't need to be out here."

"Fran's not old," Haze said.

"And she's not trying to stay in here just to do this work," Kacy added. "That's not why any of us girls are here."

"Now, you know how to speak?" Walker asked. "Haze, huh."

Why did her name sound like a dirty word coming out of his mouth? Haze skimmed over the field, checking the perimeter for Iris or Ty. She needed to speak with Clint, and the earlier, the better. She needed to see her grandmother again.

When Haze stooped to dig up more turnips, in her mind's eye she saw three men struggling near this same spot in the field. The tallest man struggled against the other two and tore away from them. He had ran a few steps before a brick struck him in back of the head. He stumbled forward and the two men rushed him again. A cloud of dust rose as the two men stomped him.

Walker moved between the rows and bent and scooped up a rutabaga. "I guess you still don't."

"Are you okay?" Kacy whispered.

"I need to talk to Iris or Ty," Haze said. Was this man in her vision in the Freemen society right now? No man in the field looked like him.

"Your eye...that thing is there again. Only a little, though."

Haze swept part of her hair over it and said, "It doesn't matter." She turned away from all of them and searched her empty pockets for something, anything.

Who could she tell about these visions? Maybe Kacy would understand?

Haze turned back to Kacy in time for the ball-sized turnip that Reed tossed at her bunkhouse mate, and Kacy ducked and sent a crooked pitch his way.

Haze jumped over the row of turnips, "I need to get some water," she said.

Walker eyeballed the small amount of vegetables in her basket and said, "This work does take a lot out of you. Bring me back a pouch."

"How come some people have water pouches?" Haze asked.

"You mean the guards, or all of them in the west and north parts?" Walker squinted at her with the sun in his face. "Guess Iris hasn't told you yet. But we're the poor ones around here. So we don't get as much food and water."

"Or women," Reed said and thrust the rake into the ground.

Walker glanced around and then took a bite out of a turnip. "You might want to get back to watching all of those kids Clint has or Wes or whoever. Keep you from being... bored."

Kacy winked at her.

"Where do the guards stay?" Haze asked, scrutinizing the handful of men in the distance for Ty's deliberate gait. "Hal is at the gate all day."

"You should've asked him that when you went to the gate," Walker replied.

Haze wiped the dirt off her face, knocked the dust off of the shapeless overalls, and said, "I'm really thirsty. I'll see if I can find Iris."

She couldn't shake the image of the dying man. Right here in these fields.

Once she'd left the field's line of sight, Haze went up one path and down another, searching for a glimpse of Ty. When she didn't find him, she circled back towards the gate for the visitor's quarters.

The small stone path had been swept clean, and that was something that her grandmother had always done. But not in the condition that Haze saw her yesterday.

When Haze arrived at the door, she took a second before opening it. No noise or sound of movement came from inside. She pushed it open, and the beds were all empty.

Haze went from bed to bed and found not one of her family's cloth sacks, no shoes, nothing. For a moment, it seemed that she had dreamed it all. They weren't here but still back in the forest and likely dead.

Haze leaned onto the bed, and a bitter taste poured into her mouth. Her stomach started to pump, but there was no food to push out. No, she wouldn't cry.

"What are you doing?" Ty said from the doorway.

CHAPTER 17

He checked behind him and left the door open.

"Ty, where's my family? Did they kick them out?"

"They moved them this morning."

"Where?

"I don't know yet."

Haze pulled him further inside and closed the door.

Ty opened it again.

Haze slammed it. "My grandmother's sick. Iris said that my family can't stay here because of the Freemen rules. Did you talk to Clint or what? I—" Haze grabbed onto the front of his jacket and said, "Ty, I can't lose them."

"I know what you mean," Ty said and slowly removed her grip, finger by finger. "Clint knows about them. So do Wes and Myles. Iris is going to take you to them."

"When?" she asked. His voice sounded as hollow as her own. It didn't seem like he'd even heard her. His stared off in the distance. "Ty? When?"

"She could be heading to the fields right now. That's where you're supposed to be, isn't it?"

"I better get going then," Haze said, and finally let go of him. Ty didn't move back from her. "Has anyone died recently? Like a man, maybe in the fields?" she asked.

Ty cocked his head. "Seven babies have died and four women. We haven't had any men die all year. Except for two of the elders, and it was their time. They'd lived over 80 jubilees," he said, and reached forward and traced the skin over her eye. "Are you really a seer?"

She jolted at the touch of his fingertips. "I don't know. Myles thinks I am," she said. The man in her vision wasn't old.

"Myles thinks a lot of things," Ty said, lowering his hand and felt for the doorknob in back of him. "I've been in here too long."

"Wait. There's something else I need."

***

Haze returned to the fields with a small pouch of water. She imagined that in the hotter months, this pouch wasn't enough for one person, let alone three or four. Just as her grandmother and mother had done the day before, Walker,

Kacy, Reed, and Camryn passed the pouch among them until it was empty.

Walker held the pouch over his mouth and squeezed out the last drop. He tossed the pouch back to her. "They always treat the new girls good," he said.

"They treat you better, Kacy?" Camryn asked.

"I wish. But I'm not new. I left and came back like the prodigal daughter," Kacy said and bowed. She straightened up. "But it can't be too bad. Before my sister died, she told me that she was on the waitlist for a better home."

"Let me guess. She died having a baby?" Camryn asked.

"Happens a lot here," Kacy said, and a shade of sadness cooled her movements.

Walker and Reed stopped picking for just a moment.

Haze inched into Kacy's shadow and carefully folded the pouch and put it in her pocket, "Has Iris been by? I thought I'd run into her before evening," she asked,

"She ain't getting dust on her clothes this early in the day," Walker replied.

Reed inched up close to her and ruffled his fingers through her bang. And like Ty before, ran his finger across her eyelid. "Besides, whatever you're asking her for, you're not getting it by breaking the rules and wandering off. Even if you are a seer."

Haze jerked her head away, wiping the dust from her face left by his dirty finger.

Camryn's cold and questioning stare came into view.

Haze grabbed the rake and swung it at him and him. "Don't do that again," she said.

Reed skitted out of the way before the handle cracked against him and nimbly leaped across the row.

"Better be careful. She'll get Myles on you," Walker said, and laughed.

Haze wanted to run away from the field, and these boys, and the Freemen society. But if she ran now, she'd be leaving her family behind.

"Leave her alone," Kacy said, and pelted them with turnips until they backed away. Then she tugged the rake from Haze's hands until she let go. "Or I'll get Ty on the both of you."

Chapter 18

Long after Haze had stopped working the field and returned to the bunkhouse with Kacy, Iris finally returned. Someone had removed the extra beds that Bailey and Trena had slept in. Either Fran or Irma used the extra space to stick more baskets next to their beds and pushed Haze's bed further into the corner.

Haze and Kacy sat inside with their jackets pulled tight.

When Iris entered the room, she shivered a moment and said, "I'll get a fire lit in here tonight. I don't know why they haven't done it already. It's like they're scared to come in here lately."

She paused at the sight of Haze, as if she weren't expecting her to be there. Haze sensed that Iris tried to read her once again.

Haze let her legs hang off the bed and swung them back and forth.

"I'm ready to visit with Camryn and Walker. Before dark-ness," Kacy said, unfolding herself from a cross-legged posi-tion.

Iris paid her no attention.

Kacy turned so that only Haze saw the right side of her face and winked. "I won't be long," she said.

Haze had already learned that the Freemen kept curfew for those under sixteen. Anyone, except the guards, roaming the community after dark was picked up and their food and water ration reduced for a quarter of a jubilee.

When the door softly clicked behind Kacy, Iris pulled the curtain aside and watched Kacy head down the path. "Her sister was the same way before she came to her senses. That kind of thing runs in families," she said.

Haze rose and went to Iris immediately and asked, "Can I see my family?"

Iris opened the door. "That's what I'm here for."

Once outside and out of earshot of Kacy, Haze asked, "So, have they decided if we can all stay?"

"No," Iris said, and the wind seemed to push her along faster than she'd ever walked. Haze had to double her pace to keep up with her. The wind whipped Haze's beaded locks into the air. "The Freemen don't break the rules."

"We won't. My grandmother needs to stay here," Haze said.

"You already have. Now tell me, where were you and your family living before Ollie brought you here?"

"In the forest," Haze replied. Had her mother or grandmother said anything? Haze grabbed Iris by the elbow, and the woman calmly faced her. "My father left us. In the forest, not the Deadwoods."

"Does Hugh belong to your father?"

Haze stepped back. "Yes, he does. Or he did. Why would you ask that?"

"So I'll know."

Haze strode ahead of her until she realized she didn't know where they were going. When Haze slowed down again, Iris wore a knowing smile.

"This way," Iris said, taking a sharp turn in the path and dipping through a hidden opening through a cluster of trees.

They met Haze's mother on the path, pacing back and forth.

Haze hurried towards her and remembered not to call her the Sisterhood name. "Mom," she said, "is grandmother better?"

Her mother's gaze swept over Iris and her as she said, "Yes, Iris brought her some herbs yesterday and this morning. She's feeling a little better."

Haze had assumed that these visitor's quarters would be better, but they weren't. The bunkhouse dwarfed these quarters yet had the same layout.

Inside, two other women roamed around, and her grandmother sat up in her bed, sipping a hot liquid with a strong garlic smell.

Haze hugged her grandmother gently and felt every bone in her back. "You look good," Haze said.

"I feel even better," her grandmother said, and her hand shook a little as she gave the cup to Haze and scrunched back against the pillows.

Haze leaned forward, hugged her again, and whispered, "Did you tell Iris or anyone about the Sisterhood?"

"Now, why would I do that?" her grandmother asked.

Relief oozed through Haze. But only a little.

Her grandmother continued, "With men, the less you say, the better. I know you don't know that. But I do. I was married once, for thirty—"

"Thirty-two years," Haze said, nodding, even though she'd never met her grandfather. He died right before she was born.

"But my daughter...I don't know about her sometimes," her grandmother said. Through the small window, Iris and Haze's mother slowly approached the quarters. Neither were speaking. Her grandmother poked her arm. "My sight isn't as good as it used to be. I thought that eye of yours looked better yesterday."

"It was," Haze said. "It's probably an infection."

"Ask that Iris woman to give you something for it."

Her mother entered the room with Iris trailing behind.

Haze asked, "Iris, can you get me something for my eye? I think it's infected."

"You think it's infected?" her mother asked, and her mouth tightened.

"It's infected," Haze replied.

Iris checked the floors and around the other women's beds. She took a basket off the bed, returned it to the floor, and said, "I'll get you something for it." She approached the three of them. "I can really see the resemblance. Bernice, I can only imagine how many suitors you had at Haze's age."

Haze's grandmother threw back her head and laughed. "I can see that here my granddaughters' got the same opportunities," she said, settling back against the pillows again.

Haze couldn't hide her surprise at her grandmother's delight about these opportunities.

Haze's mother also laughed a little and asked, "Can my daughter get that medicine for her eye before tonight?"

"Absolutely," Iris said and turned to leave.

"Give you something else to do besides smile," her mother said in a low voice.

Haze sagged inside. Her mother didn't like it here. Even though she hadn't been here long, something in her was set against it. She'd been the same way with the Sisterhood in the beginning and right through the end.

"Haze?" Iris called her from outside and tapped the window.

Haze knew what phrase came next.

"Come now."

Chapter 19

Haze hugged her grandmother and mother again before meeting Iris outside.

"What kind of medicine do the Freemen have?" she asked.

The fast clip that Iris had done on their trip over to the visitor's quarter had disappeared. Haze followed her up one winding path and down another.

The Sisterhood had a healer who had been a nurse before the Destruction, and any sickness didn't last long.

"That's not my area of expertise," Iris said.

"What is your area?"

"You sure ask a lot of questions, honey. So does your mom. But I make sure things run smoothly," Iris said, and something around her neck caught the pale sunlight. "And here we are."

Haze fully expected her to sweep her arm out as if showing something grand. Instead, Iris led her to the backyard of the small green home, which had small jars lining the path rather than lanterns.

"Millie," Iris said to the older woman on her knees in the dirt and deftly digging a small hole next to a bed of plants. "This young lady here needs something for her eye. She has an infection that created a frighteningly thick wad of skin."

Millie wore the same type of overalls that Haze and the other women had on earlier, except hers were midnight blue, and she chewed on a dandelion sprig.

Haze immediately recognized aloe and yarrow plants, among others in the yard.

Millie stopped digging and shaded her eyes as she looked up and said, "Back again so soon? I thought I wouldn't see you until tomorrow." Millie stood, and she had to be around Haze's grandmother's age but with far more energy. "What do I call you?"

"Her name's Haze," Iris said.

"I'm sure she could've told me that," Millie said.

"Her grandmother's the one that had your medicine yesterday and again this morning," Iris said. She nudged Haze. "Right honey?"

"How long has that eye been like that?" Millie asked. She spit out the sprig, and Iris winced. "Do you mind if I take a better look?"

"It just started a few days ago," Haze replied, lifting her chin a little as Millie peered closer.

"Did it? It doesn't seem so bad," the older woman said. "Come with me. Let's see what I can muster up. Iris, if you can watch that area over there, which has my tobacco plants, I'd much appreciate it. Don't want the men wandering in and picking through it."

Iris gave a strained laugh and said, "Of course."

Haze followed Millie into her house and entered through the sunny kitchen.

Inside, glass jars lined each shelf with small herbs growing out of it.

"You're new. How did you find us?" Millie asked and took out three small jars from a cabinet above next to the largest window.

Haze ran a fingertip along the wood. Hand carved, she could tell. "I didn't. The Freemen found me."

"Come. Sit," Millie said, tapping the chair by the window. She opened the first jar as Haze seated herself. "Found you where?"

"Near the forest. But not the Deadwoods."

"You weren't there long. Nothing good grows there. Where were you before?"

"All I know is the forest."

"And yet you have the posture of a girl raised by the Sisterhood."

"The what?" she asked. Haze flinched and then flinched again at the sting of the cream applied near her eye. She had practiced answering nosy questions about her whereabouts growing up if asked by Myles or Clint or Iris.

"How do you like it here so far?" Millie asked and popped open the second jar. A pungent smell sliced through the air.

Haze shifted in her seat, her eyes watering from the pungent smell. "It's different," she said. "Lots of men."

"Ahh, the Deadwoods are stacked with men, too. The kind you're scared to turn your back on or look'em in the eye if you're face'em. Now, this last one's going to sting a bit."

Haze braced herself as Millie slid the salve over the rough skin, yet felt a rush of coolness. "It only stings if you don't like it," she said. "I heard that a girl with a funny eye helped deliver a baby the other day."

"That was me. I helped Clint's wife."

Millie raised an eyebrow and said, "Which one?"

"Amie," Haze said, and stifled a laugh.

Millie wiped her hands on a cloth and said, "That's some good schooling you had. In the forest, not the Deadwoods." She lifted a lock of Haze's hair with tiny blue and green beads woven through it, smiled, and laid it back down again. "Delivering babies from those men."

Haze squirmed out of the chair. "My eye's starting to feel better already," she said.

"Is it?" Millie asked and ushered Haze back to the door. "Then I've done my job."

"Now I won't feel so bad when I see Myles and the others."

Millie immediately shut the door. "What does Myles want with you?" she asked. Her brows knitted together like an angry mountain.

"He—I asked to see Clint, but I know Myles and Wes will be there too. Since I got here, I don't know, but Myles has been—"

"What, child?"

"He's been on me about being a seer. When it's just some kind of infection."

"How old are you?"

A hollowness filled Haze, "Thirteen," she said, before something in her cracked. "Fifteen."

"Being a seer isn't your biggest worry. Not with that man." Millie said and went to her cabinet and returned with a small blue bottle the size of Haze's thumb. "Before you see them. Drink this. Not as soon as you get there, but while you're still where you sleep. It'll help your eye even more. Put it away for now."

Haze hid the bottle inside her jacket pocket.

Millie opened the door again.

A small crowd of men trailed across the path outside her backyard. Some of the men shouted greetings to Millie.

Still in the backyard, Iris spoke with animation with one of the men. Haze made sure to tuck the bottle into the folds of the jacket as she approached Iris and her prying eyes.

Iris's laugh somersaulted through the backyard. When she saw Haze and Millie, she composed herself.

The man turned around, and Haze's breath caught in her chest as if she'd been struck.

Millie's yard and all its surrounding space disappeared for a moment. Haze clapped her hand over her good eye for a moment, willing it to see things right.

It wasn't the man's brown skin or flat nose that made it seem as if time had stopped. That was many of the Freemen. Nor his hooded and deep-set eyes. It was his crooked front teeth, like her own.

Haze's father straightened his posture when he saw her.

Chapter 20

The sturdy wooden fence rose to the height of Iris's hips. She rested against it for a moment longer, watching the men pass.

Haze quickly dropped her hand before Iris turned around.

Millie navigated around Haze as the wave of men continued to tramp by and said to Iris, "I'm done. Now I can go back to my work."

Iris carefully examined Haze as she approached. She waved off Haze's father and said, "I'll see you at home."

Haze's father slowly backed away, grim-faced, until he turned and disappeared down the path.

"My goodness, Haze. You look a fright," Iris said. "Come now, I know Millie can't be that bad."

"My eye—it stings," Haze said, forcing out the words. How long had her father been here? How come she'd never seen him in a vision, just these other men who meant nothing to her? "Was that your husband, Iris?"

"You're a smart girl, Haze," Iris replied, pulling out the necklace buried inside her shirt, and a thin gold ring dangled from it.

Millie picked up her gardening tool and said, "Bring her by again in a day or two. So I can see how things have developed."

On the way back to the bunkhouse, Haze asked, "How long've you been married?"

"Six jubilees," she said, "and he's my second one."

"You have children with him?" Haze asked, wondering if she should tell her mother or let them run into each other.

"Mine are grown. And he didn't want any, which worked for me," Iris said, and waved to a man about Ty's age across the path, who was arm-in-arm with a girl no older than Haze. "See that? She's already 17. She came here last jubilee. They married last quarter."

"Good for her," Haze replied and wished she didn't care that her father had come this way, but she did. She wished she hadn't seen him with Iris. How could he leave her mother? Leave her and Hugh and come here? And never look back.

"I hope it lasts."

"If it doesn't, she'll have another waiting if she's smart. Your mother told me yesterday that she and your grandmother raised you and your brother all by themselves," Iris said, and there was a sense of wonderment to her voice and something else.

Haze's mind racing with thoughts. "Is your husband from here?" she finally asked as they neared the bunkhouse.

"He's not," Iris said, tucking her necklace back into her shirt and coat.

"How long has he been here?"

"Honey, you ask so many questions. If I didn't know any better, I'd think you were part of the Council."

Haze gave a weak laugh in unison with Iris's chuckle.

Iris held the bunkhouse door open for Haze, examining her eye in the split second that Haze passed by her.

The warmth from the fireplace, along with the lanterns, lit the inside. Iris didn't come inside the bunkhouse, nor did she tell Haze anything more about whether her family could stay.

Kacy scoured under her bed and then Fran's. "I lost my earring," she said. "You have all those little jewels in your hair. Maybe I can use one of those."

"You can," Haze said, unfastening one of the tiny jewels from her hair. Since she no longer belonged to the Sisterhood what difference did it make.

Kacy quickly said, "I was just kidding."

"I don't mind."

"No, seriously. These were my sister's earrings, so I need to find the other one."

Haze refastened the jewel. Did her hair give away her origin? "You ever seen anyone else with these jewels and beads?"

"Can't say I have," Kacy said, dumping the clothes out of the basket and onto the bed. Yet her eyes flicked in Haze's direction. "But I've heard that some groups do their hair like that."

"What kind of groups?"

Kacy maneuvered so that she was sideways, and Haze couldn't see her face and shrugged. "Just different groups. I've heard that women have societies too, just like this one. Or something like it, and there used to be a lot of them, but not so much anymore."

"I heard that too."

Kacy looked her in the eye and said, "Well, I think you need to keep what you heard to yourself. The Freemen won't let in women from those groups. Girls either, over the age of twelve. Half of the women in those groups were probably kicked out of a place like this or just hated it and left."

Haze picked an emerald-green scarf from the small pile of clothes and said, "Iris took me to see an herbalist about my eye."

"It's looking kinda shiny from here. Millie's really good at what she does."

"I know, and Iris called her an herbalist when she's really a healer."

Kacy's head jerked. "Myles is the holy man and the healer. So there's no place for Millie to be a healer," she said. "That's one more thing you don't need to mention to anyone else."

"Is Ty from here?"

Haze didn't have to turn around to know that Kacy was smiling.

"Born and raised a Freemen. Why?" Kacy asked.

Haze felt her face grow warm and said, "I was just asking."

"I know."

"He's so much younger than Hal and the other guards."

"He's got better chances, too."

"Of being a guard?"

Kacy snickered. "No, of getting a wife. Hal's days for that are over. And the only thing he's married to is being a guard and that homebrew he sips while on guard. Was like that when I was here the first time. Nothing has changed."

"So, why did you come back?"

"I don't want to be alone out there," Kacy said, pawing at the small hoop earring caught inside the basket and putting it back in her ear. And before Haze could say it, "I wouldn't last in some place full of nothing but other girls. Maybe if I were Millie's age. Probably not even then."

"Same for me. But only if the leadership is rotten. Then everything it touches rots," Haze said, carefully removing her jacket. She palmed the small bottle and hid it in under her covers. "My family built their own shelter."

"So what?" she asked and dropped her voice to a whisper. Fran and Irma's laughter whirled up the path as they approached the bunkhouse. Kacy shuddered as if the laughter hurt her. "Your granny's not going to last forever, and neither will your mom. Especially not in the Deadwoods. I've been through there. The outskirts. Not deep in it. You don't want to stay out there till you're Fran and Irma's age. Your best chance is right here."

Chapter 21

Unlike the bunkhouse rugs, the Sanctuary's hallway rugs were tightly woven by hand. Not that it mattered. The men had left wet footprints across it. Iris hurried them down the hall towards the Council's room.

Haze silently panicked. She hadn't taken Millie's medicine before she left the bunkhouse this morning. Iris had wanted to beat the rain showers. No time for Haze to detour and check in on her grandmother and get some words to help convince the Council to let them stay.

Haze coughed and coughed again. Within seconds, she bent over double, coughing violently. Iris tapped her on the back several times.

"Hold on," Iris said and disappeared around the corner. She returned seconds later carrying a cup of water.

Wes opened the Council's door. "Is this happening today or not?" he asked Iris.

"Haze," Iris said, "hurry now. Everyone's waiting."

Turning her back to them, Haze palmed the small blue bottle and poured it into the glass of water. She gulped it. And immediately gagged as the bitter taste spilled own her throat. The liquid seeped from the corners of her mouth, sloshing down her neck.

Iris took Haze by the shoulders and spun her around.

The taste of the medicine mingled with the scent of the crushed gardenia flowers that Iris used daily.

Haze blinked, trying to clear her vision.

Did her father like that scent? Her mother never had time to perfume herself.

"How's your eye?" Iris said and the smile nearly died on her lips. "I'd better get you in front of them."

She smoothed Haze's lock partially over her face so that it swung over her eye.

Haze took a deep breath and followed Iris into the room, where the three men positioned themselves at a circular table with eight chairs. A woman in tears brushed past them out of the room.

Haze's mother was also seated at the table with her back towards the door and facing the giant windows. The wind whipped through the trees and shook the windows.

Was this supposed to be some long line of no's?

"Have a seat," Wes said, and Iris pulled out the chair for Haze and then returned to stand near the door as she had each time before. Haze fidgeted, elbow-to-elbow with her mother.

"Thea," Wes said, and his gaze flitted between Myles and Clint before he spoke again. "Can I call you that?"

Haze scraped the chair against the floor at the sound of her mother's name. She hadn't heard it in years.

"Maybe," Haze's mother said.

Clint seemed fixated by the architecture of the room.

Myles rested his chin in his hand and drummed his fingers to a beat only he heard.

Wes continued, "Your daughter has been a big help to my friend here and his wife. And because of that, we want to make sure that we give you a fair chance."

"But we must follow the rules," Myles said quickly. "The Freemen society has open membership every seven jubilees for 13 weeks. Your daughter came the last three days of the jubilee. You and your mother came the day after it closed. Your daughter has asked us to permit you and your mother to stay—"

"But I didn't ask," Haze's mother said. Despite her words, the hard edge to her voice when she addressed Iris wasn't there for these men.

"Sis—Mom?" Haze said and stood.

Wes frowned as she loomed over him.

Haze cleared her throat and said, "Grandmother is sick. She can't go back to the forest. We can't go back there."

The desk seemed to tilt and move beneath her fingertips and Haze seated herself again. Sweat prickled on her forehead.

"What's so important about the Freemen? Besides that, you have my daughter working for all of your women, and I can't see my son," Haze's mother said.

Haze's vision blurred and three Clints, two Myles and three Wes's surrounded the table. But no father. She hadn't had the chance to tell her mother yet.

"Mom," Haze said.

"We were in the forest or woods or whatever you call it and I kept my children fed and clothed. You took my children and made me come here. This trip nearly killed my mother. She can't walk. She's barely eaten the few scraps that you've given us," Haze's mother said.

"Our guards found your daughter and son sick. We brought him here. Your daughter came on her own. We have no problem with that because the Freemen are always willing to accept more women members. We have a lot of men here that need wives," Clint said.

"Maybe if the men's leaders stop marrying so many women, the rest of the men'd have one," Haze's mother said.

Iris coughed as if something had caught in her throat.

Clint stopped speaking for a moment. He leaned back in his chair and rubbed his chin.

The wind crashed against the building harder than ever.

Wes jumped to his feet as if he'd heard invisible instructions and said, "I'll have the guards escort you out of the gate today."

"No! Please," Haze said, twisting in the seat away from the window, which sounded like it might shatter any moment. "Please don't. There's a bad storm coming. My grandmother will die."

"We have storms like this every jubilee," Myles said. "What makes you think this one is bad?"

"I've lived through enough of them," Haze said.

"Do you know your daughter's a seer?" Myles asked Haze's mother. "Seers are supposed to be male."

Haze's mother said, "She's not one. She's a smart girl. As smart as any boy, whether he's a seer or a guard."

"She is a seer, but that's not important," Myles said, rising from his chair and strolling to the window. "What is important is that the three of us must agree to change these rules for you to stay. I want your daughter to tell me what she see's coming with this storm."

"I told you before--" Haze said.

"That was before," Clint said. "Did you know you'd help deliver my daughter? Did you know that she'd...live?"

Haze clumsily unclipped a small jewel from her hair and pushed it across the table at him. "You just needed a midwife. My grandmother is one, and she taught me," she said.

"If she refuses to tell the truth, then she must go. Her brother can stay. But not her or the women who taught her to behave this way," Myles said, and removed three white pebbles from his pocket and stacked them on the windowsill.

The wind outside made everything tilt, or maybe it was whatever was in that blue bottle.

"What's important is that you're lying about your rules. What's important is that some of your people hate you. What's important is that some leaders shouldn't be leaders," Haze said, weakly, and rose from her seat. "Mom, we need to get out of here."

She leaned on her mother, who helped her wobble towards the door, which Iris opened.

Iris came into the hallway with them.

"Haze, young lady. You're full of surprises," Iris said, and the shattering of glass and the roar from the men still in the room punctuated her words.

Chapter 22

Wes and Clint rolled from underneath the overturned table. Myles held his hand to his forehead and blood seeped from between his fingers. Yet he still managed to glare at Haze when she peeked around the corner and into the room.

Shattered glass covered the floor. This was why the Sisterhood didn't have glass.

"You're going to tell me she didn't know that was coming?" Myles asked the other two men.

"No, she didn't," her mother said. "She's not responsible for a grown man's choice to stand next to a window.

"Myles," Wes said, "do we need to get Fred? He may need to stitch you up."

Haze guessed that Fred was the one restraining Amie the other night while she struggled to deliver her baby alive.

Myles used the edge of his shirt to mop the blood from his face.

A loud piercing sound wailed through the open window and made the hair rise along Haze's neck.

"What's that?" Haze asked.

The wind sucked the blankets that functioned as curtains out of the window, and Haze wished that Myles went with it.

Iris herded them back into the hallway. "It's the siren. I haven't heard it in three or four jubilees. We need to stay right here."

"Why?" Haze's mother asked.

"A tornado or something must be happening. Maybe someone's hurt or a lightning fire."

"What?" Haze's mother said. "My mother is still in your visitor's quarters, and she's alone. And I don't know where my son is. You people won't let him stay with me."

"They're safe right where they are," Clint said from the doorway, shaking the glass fragments from his clothes. "You can stay here. But I need to check on my family."

"So do I," Haze's mother said, pushing Haze down the hallway. Haze resisted and her mother pushed harder. "Go find your brother. Make sure he's safe."

"What if he's already safe?" Haze asked.

"You don't know that."

Haze opened the front door, and the wind knocked her backwards into her mother.

When Haze looked back, Clint motioned for her to return to the hallway. "Maybe I should wait?" she asked.

"You can't. Don't be scared," her mother pushed her back towards the door. "I'm going to your grandmother. I can't believe this is happening, and she's by herself."

Haze wanted to say that grandmother had been by herself through a lot of things and usually turned out better than before.

Instead she fought her way through the powerful wind while her mother went in the opposite direction. She had an idea of where Hugh stayed.

The cold, white rain came hard and sudden when Haze was sure she was near the children's quarters. It soaked her to the bone and flooded the paths so that she couldn't see a thing.

For some time, she huddled in the doorway of a gray colored building waiting for the worst of it to blow over. No one passed by. She couldn't stay here forever and a part of her wished that she had stayed at the Sanctuary where she would be safe and dry.

But that was selfish. She needed to check on Hugh.

Someone needed to check Myles. She hadn't given him the answer that he wanted, which meant either she'd have to face their council again or get kicked out or both.

If she had such vision, then why didn't she know that her father was here? How come she hadn't seen him in any vision ever? And she had waited to see him for years, wondering if he'd ever find them in the Deadwoods and even when they moved to the Sisterhood.

Haze had never known anyone that was a seer or what they did or saw. No one had ever told her that only boys could be seers. The Sisterhood had never mentioned it and they'd spoken of the gifts of womanhood almost at every meal.

She never had to worry about her hair or how she looked in the Sisterhood. But she had to watch her words there too. The Sisterhood wanted no talk of men and their ways except the occasional mention of a child's father.

But despite the discussions of womanhood, Haze had heard other conversations too from the older women, the women that were young long before The Destruction.

The Sisterhood shrank a little each year as the founding members died off and the younger ones had one child or none at all. Siblings were rare and Haze was one of the few that had one.

A spear of lightning flashed through the sky directly overhead.

Haze restrained herself from dashing back to the Sanctuary. Haze knew from snatches of conversation that she'd find the children's quarters near the north gate.

When the downpour and fierce winds didn't subside, Haze pushed back into it again until she found her way towards the wall and followed it. She sloshed through the path with the water at her ankles.

But the rain came even harder until Haze couldn't see in front of her. But she knew she was near the guard station.

Tree branches blew by her and floated in the large puddles. Something struck her shoulder and Haze put her arms over her head. When she got to the door, the wind pushed her so hard that she slammed against it.

One of the guards opened the station door. "Christ almighty," he said, and shepherded her inside. Haze welcomed the warmth as the water from her clothes pooled at her feet.

Ty turned from his post.

"Haze? What are you doing?" he said, coming over to her.

Haze squeezed the rain from her sweater and wiped the water streaming down her face. Both Ty and the other guard led her to a chair to sit down.

Haze struggled to catch her breath. "I need to check on Hugh," she said.

"Did something happen to him?" Ty asked.

"I don't know. This is such an awful storm."

Ty had leaned over her and now straightened up and said, "he's with the other kids. Not out roaming around like you. This place floods sometimes. You shouldn't be out there."

"My mother told me to find Hugh. And I still haven't. Can you take me to him?"

"When the storm is over."

Haze thought about it for a heartbeat. "Forget it. I'll find him myself," she said, and rose from the chair so quickly, she almost head-butted the other guard. The dizziness that she'd felt earlier at the Sanctuary returned.

"Hey," the guard said. As soon as Haze opened the door a crack, the wind blew it open so that it slammed against the wall. "Wait a minute. You shouldn't go out there alone."

"I'm used to it," Haze said, over her shoulder.

In the few minutes that she'd been inside, the water had pooled even more in spots, and the white rain continued, but the powerful wind had almost stopped.

Haze took a deep breath and unzipped her jacket. The road in front of her blurred for just a moment, and Haze waited for the blurriness to pass.

She struggled up the slanted road towards the small, flat building that reminded her of the schoolrooms that she'd seen in the Sisterhood's books. Her arms and legs grew heavier and heavier with each step.

Lightning crackled through the sky, followed by a thunderbolt that zapped the tree ahead of her.

Haze screamed as the tree split, and a huge chunk crashed over the path up ahead. She darted away at the force of the tree hitting the ground and the effort made her dizzier. Everything in sight split into two, three, four things.

Haze's knees buckled, and she tried not to fall into the puddle, but lost consciousness before she hit the ground. The rain continued to pelt.

Someone had her by the arms. No, she was being carried. A chorus of young boys choppy singing drowned out the rain and wind.

Haze opened her eyes as she passed under a doorway and met Ty's dark gaze.

Inside, a circle of twenty or so six-, seven-, and eight-year-old boys continued singing and fidgeting on a large rug.

A man and woman, both with guitars, sat cross-legged at the head of the circle. Hugh didn't see her. He was busy singing off-key along with the other boys.

Haze closed her eyes for a second and whispered, "My brother. I came to check on my brother."

She'd tell her grandmother about this scene and that Hugh didn't seem to miss them too much.

The guitar couple kept playing to keep the boys' attention, but the woman pointed to a comfy chair in the corner of the room.

Ty plopped her down in it, and water squished from her clothes on the chair.

Hugh play-boxed with another boy before turning and facing her.

"Haze," he said, and ran over to her. "You're all wet," he said and hugged her still. In the few days they'd been there, his face had filled a little more from getting food every day. He dug into his pocket and pulled out a small wooden instrument. "Look what I got? I bet you don't know what this is?"

"Looks like a funny comb," Haze said.

Ty leaned against the wall. Silent.

"It's a harmonica," Hugh said and blew into it with every ounce of breath in his lungs. Haze felt herself shrink inside just a little. Hugh had never been so happy.

"Next song," the woman said, strumming the guitar. "Hugh, start us off."

Hugh ran back over and found his seat again.

Ty hadn't moved.

She knew better than to mention leaving, but maybe Ty needed to. She drew her knees up to her chest. "Are you going to stay here until the storm's over?" she asked him without taking her eyes off the kids.

"I have to stand watch on the perimeters," Ty said, pivoted, and seemed to take in the position of the other people. Was this the men's ways that the Sisterhood spoke about? He leaned towards her, and Haze thought he was reaching for her hand.

He placed the small blue bottle into her palm and said, "This fell out of your pocket when I picked you up."

Chapter 23

Haze put the warm bottle back into her pocket. She wanted to pretend that she didn't know what Ty meant. But she had no idea what happened when she lost consciousness.

"It was something for my eye," she said.

He scanned the room again, especially the door. No one in the room paid them any mind.

"I've seen bottles like that before. No one used it on their eye."

"What did you use it for?" she asked.

"I haven't, and I don't need to. I'm a Freemen and I only deal with reality. Not fairy tales or wishes. Or visions."

Haze sucked in her breath.

The woman continued playing the guitar, and the man came over to them.

"Is there a problem, Ty?" he asked.

He didn't have the suspicious gaze of Myles, but his confident stride reminded her of Clint.

"She wanted to see her brother and got lost in the storm," Ty replied.

Haze waited for the man's reaction when he caught sight of her eye and there was none. He held out his hand and said, "I'm Gus. That's my sister Velma over there."

Haze limply shook it. Did Ty mean that he believed she had visions? She hadn't told anyone about them. She didn't know what to believe. Haze lowered her chin.

"Did you want to join us?" Gus asked Haze.

Haze kept her head down.

"Next time I come here, Gus, I expect to hear drums too," Ty said.

Gus chuckled and said, "Hal made us stop. Said he heard the drums all the way to the gate. Did you want to join us?"

Haze shook her head, and Gus returned to the circle.

"I think the rain's stopped," Haze said, absently rubbing her good eye.

She'd find her way back to the bunkhouse and let the last of the dizzy feeling drain out. And find out if her bunkmates fared better than she did. She hoped her mother had made it safely back to the visitor's quarters.

"I'll send Iris for you," Ty replied. "Bury that bottle in the field. Or else Myles will come for you."

Haze jarred as if thunder crackled. "I'm not scared of Myles," she said, a lump rising in her throat.

Ty tilted his head slightly.

"Should I be?" she asked.

"The Council sets the rules. They decide what man stays and what man is forced out. Which man gets a wife and which one doesn't."

"That's not fair."

"Where have you lived that fairness is part of the rules?"

Haze opened her mouth and shut it so hard her teeth clicked.

"Bury the bottle. Until then, you have Gus and Velma to entertain you."

Chapter 24

Iris arrived much later that afternoon to escort Haze back to the bunkhouse. Not a bird sang or a person moved on the waterlogged land beside her and this woman. She wanted to tell Iris that she'd gone to the children's quarters alone, well, almost alone. She didn't need a chaperone everywhere she went.

In the Sisterhood, she'd gone where she pleased. But she wasn't a true member of the Freemen yet.

"Has the council asked about me?" Haze asked, sidestepping another pool of water and using the opportunity to switch to the other side of Iris and side-view the woman with her good eye. The veil blocked her peripheral vision. "What've you told them?"

Iris's expression didn't change. "They haven't asked anything outside the norm. How old are you? Where did you come from? Do you look healthy and fertile? Did you come alone or with others?"

"What did they say?" Haze asked when Iris didn't offer any more details. She seemed unusually quiet and far less bubbly.

Iris seemed to realize that Haze watched her and perked up. "Well, honey, you're young and your mom's still on your side of young and fertile, so you may have a chance. Some of the girls that've come here over the years have been drinking that water out there. The boys too. It messes them up. But," she hesitated, "I don't think they like this eye issue you have. Or your mother."

"My mom hasn't been here long," Haze replied, wondering if Iris was joking. The Sisterhood had liked her mom, except for Phoenyx. It was her grandmother they never liked and often told to stop talking about her marriage from years ago.

Kacy, Fran, and Irma met them on the water-filled path to the bunkhouse.

"Part of the roof's gone," Fran said. "We can't stay there."

"All of our stuff's all wet," Kacy said and had her blanket wrapped around her shoulders. "The day's been horrible. I'm already freezing."

"I should've known this would happen. Our other visitor's quarter was damaged today too," Iris said.

"The one with my grandmother?" Haze asked, and her voice rose several octaves.

Iris nodded. "I have one other place for you."

Haze scouted out places to drop the bottle away from Iris's eagle eye vision as she led them towards the western part of the community. This area had more trees and less homes. And the surrounding land didn't have as many ditches and pooling water. Clint's home, which sat on a hill, was somewhere in the vicinity.

This visitor quarter was the same size as the bunkhouse and had more beds. Haze's grandmother and mother were already in the first room. Walker and Reeds' voices drummed through the walls from the adjoining room.

Kacy nudged Haze with an elbow and didn't bother to hide her grin.

Haze mouthed the word, no. No way was she sharing her space with any males.

"Haze?" Her grandmother called out.

"Grandmother," Haze said, throwing her arms out and hurrying over. Her grandmother, who had the biggest bed and the thickest blankets, played cards with another older woman. She wrapped her arms around her grandmother and pressed her cheek against her grandmother's wrinkles.

"They moved me here last night," her grandmother said, and pat the space on the bed next to her for Haze to sit. Haze loved the way her grandmother looked at her, always with warmth. "I heard that storm, but I didn't feel it."

Haze's mother flipped through some sort of book. Grandmother had made sure that her daughter and Haze knew how to read, even though no one did it much.

"Sis--, mom was worried about you. We left the Council during the storm. I went to find Hugh," Haze said, and squeezed in between the beds.

"That boy is just fine. Are you?" she asked and put down her card immediately. She folded Haze into a hug. The other women flipped a card and gleefully took all of her grandmother's cards. "You should've stayed put, like your mother."

"Mom didn't stay. She left with me."

Haze's mother closed the book and said, "It was too much for me, so I turned around and went back. Did you find your brother?"

"Yes, and he was happy with the other kids. And dry. I almost got hurt out there," Haze said and decided not to mention that Ty had been there to help her.

Haze's mother took a sip from a mug of hot liquid. "I was worried about you. I thought about going after you," she said.

"But you didn't," Haze's grandmother said. "I certainly wouldn't have sent Haze out there alone."

Haze's mother reached over and cupped Haze's face. "Iris, I thought you'd gotten Haze some medicine for her eye. It looks worse than ever. This thing is huge. It looks bigger than this morning."

Haze groaned inward at the stares from the other women. Walker and Reed immediately appeared in the doorway of the adjoining room.

"Kacy and Haze. Haze and Kacy," Reed said, with a leisurely and lingering gaze from Haze's feet, hips, breasts, skipped over her face, and went down her body again.

Haze had dried up somewhat at the children's quarters thanks to the fireplace, but her clothes were still damp and clung to her body.

Both boys, though, were bone dry. And their clothes emitted a woodsy scent that Haze couldn't identify.

Iris came towards Haze and her mother, mouth pressed into a tight line. "She may need another application."

"I do," Haze said, swiftly, buttoning up the wet jacket. Walker winked, but at Kacy, not her. "The herbalist didn't give me anymore to use."

"Herbalist? Is that what she's called here? Well, she sure has done me right," Her grandmother said. "Haze, you need to get out of those wet clothes."

"Yeah, Haze," Reed said with a snicker.

Walker quickly elbowed Reed in the ribs.

"Why are you speaking to my daughter?" Haze's mother asked Reed.

"He didn't mean it," Walker said.

Haze's grandmother scooped up the other women's cards and said, "Iris, it's getting late. Shouldn't these young men head to wherever they're staying?"

Iris's gaze shifted from Haze's mother to Haze and then over to Kacy, Walker and Reed. "It's too crowded for all of you here. Haze, Kacy, I'll settle you somewhere else."

"What? Where?" Kacy said, with her mouth poked out.

"There ain't nowhere else," Walker said.

"We'll stay in that other room," Reed added.

"I believe that Clint has space in his home," Iris said firmly.

"Is that the one from this morning?" Haze's mother said and blocked Iris's path. "The one with all of the wives? He's—"

"Thea," Haze's grandmother said sharply. "His wives may have something for Haze's eye and a change of clothes."

Kacy wrapped the blanket around her shoulders again, and Walker and Reed stomped back into the adjoining room.

Haze's mother settled back into the bed and sat as if she had a rod inserted in her back. Haze went to hug her mother. Her mother immediately crossed her arms but leaned forward. Haze wanted to drop the small bottle between the covers, but the old woman and Iris watched her.

"Come now. It's getting late," Iris said.

And she needs to get home to my father, Haze wanted to say.

Chapter 25

Lily steered them out of the messy living space and toward the children's quarters at the opposite end of the hallway. "I knew you'd bring them here. I keep this room prepared. You'll find fresh clothes in it."

Four lanterns lit the cozy room. Clint's children played in the next room and thumped against the walls.

Haze pulled off the damp sweater, and leaves came from underneath. She still had the bottle hidden in her jacket because the pants had no pockets.

"What in the world?" Kacy said as crumbled leaves fluttered to the floor.

"I fell down the path during the storm."

"And you rolled into a pile of leaves at the bottom?"

Haze burst into laughter, and it felt good because she hadn't laughed in a long time. She was going to spend the night in Clint and Lily's house, and she wasn't afraid at all.

"Kacy, I don't know what boy you'll marry, but he's going to have his hands full."

Kacy made sure the door was closed. "You know it," she said. "I heard you and your grandma talking. Next time, stay inside. I know you saw the Council again. They had coffee and water and whatever you needed at the Sanctuary."

"They didn't say yes to my family staying though," Haze said and rummaged through the clothes.

"They're still here, aren't they? If they didn't want you, they wouldn't have opened the gate to begin with. You know how many men are visiting the Council to land you as their wife when you turn sixteen? I told you yesterday that you need to play this right."

"I never said I wanted marriage."

"You never said you didn't."

"Girls," Lily said from the other side of the door. "Come into the living space. I have something to show you."

Kacy entered the living space first, with Haze behind her. Haze smiled at the small gurgling sound before she saw the tiny baby. Clint, Amie, and Lily had placed the baby on a small cushion in the middle of the living space, and they sat in a circle around it while the fireplace crackled nearby.

"Her name's Nyomi," Amie said, and she also had a cushion underneath her.

"She's beautiful," Kacy said.

"All babies are beautiful," Haze said.

"How many others have you helped deliver?" Lily asked. "Have you had one yourself?"

"I haven't," Haze said, aware that Clint watched her closely. "Nyomi's the only one I've delivered myself. But I've helped the midwives before."

"What midwives?" Amie asked. "I thought that knowledge was destroyed with the Destruction."

Kacy stared at Haze wide-eyed with nostrils flaring. "My grandmother still has that knowledge," Haze said.

"But you said midwives, so it was someone else besides your grandmother," Amie said.

"I heard her say midwife," Lily said, stretching her back. She leaned against the cushions and balanced an empty cup on her belly. "Haze, can you get me some water from the barrel? It'll take me forever to stand up."

Haze took the empty pitcher and escaped the room. Outside, at the water barrel, she drank some herself, the cold water soothing her dry throat, before filling the pitcher for Lily.

A clear, fat, moon stared down at her. Far off, a pack of dogs howled. Here, she didn't have to scour for water day in and day out.

Haze returned with the pitcher while Kacy riveted them with her words.

"It was terrible. I was scared to sleep at night. I never knew who was around. There were some friendly ones, but most weren't," Kacy said.

Clint held Nyomi and rocked her a little. "What about you, Haze? What were you doing before Ty found you and Hugh?"

Haze could almost hear Kacy's silent words of warning. "Just helping my mom and grandmother take care of Hugh. I had to set traps, and we tried to grow food."

"A young woman needs something to do besides setting traps and hunting," Lily said.

Haze nodded. "I was lonely most of the time."

"Hugh's about six or seven," Clint said. "Did you know your father?"

"He left when I was about Hugh's age. I woke up one morning, and he was gone," Haze said, with as even a tone as possible. The years of wondering if he was dead or alive had meant nothing.

"All the more reason for Haze and her family to stay here," Kacy said.

"It's good that you're used to this type of structure. Some girls aren't. Or boys. They want to come in here, yet they're full of rebellion for this life," Amie said. "I've been born and raised here. I can't imagine any other type of life."

"I had it and believe me this is a lot better. Now if the Council allowed women, we could really improve this place," Lily said and double-winked at Haze and Kacy.

"I've suggested it to Myles before and he's against it," Clint said. "He's said many times that what's important is that the Council remains united."

Haze's eye started to itch, and it hadn't in days. "What's important?" she asked. "Myles said that this morning. So it's important that the Council not take women's counsel?"

Clint didn't miss a beat. "Of course not. There's not a Freemen here whose wife or sister or mother doesn't have his ear."

"And his sanity," Lily said, and the three of them laughed and Kacy joined in.

For Haze, a vision unfolded at Clint's words. Five men and two women cloaked by the shadows near the wall. Haze saw none of their faces, just their outlines and as the men passed the woman something inside a small sack like the one Haze had.

"Myles doesn't believe that," Haze said, feeling almost tipsy with the vision, which allowed words she hadn't meant to speak, out. And from the sober expressions around her, she knew her words were a mistake.

CHAPTER 26

Haze's words flamed through the air much like the fire from days before. Lily's shoulders sank. Amie's mouth tightened. Kacy shut her eyes for a brief moment. The fire embers hissed.

Amie immediately took Nyomi from Clint's arms.

Kacy and Clint spoke simultaneously.

"She's kidding," Kacy said, and gave a weak laugh.

Clint folded his hands in front of him and asked, "What would make you say that?"

"Myles has…" Haze said and searched for the words and avoided Kacy's blazing stare. The slow howl of the wind outside had picked up again. "He's not just doing things with the Council. He talks to other people outside this community."

"We all do that. We have to," Clint said. "They're other communities around besides this one. They're not as well-run and they don't have our resources either. We have a warm spring that runs through this land and gives us fresh, clean water. People kill for water. That's what caused the Destruction."

"It's not just about the water," Haze said, resisting the urge to claw at her itching eye. None of the men in that vision appeared to have the physique of Myles or Wes or Clint. What if what she was seeing was wrong?

Clint stood and paced the room. "Haze, this is something that I'll have to report. You've made a serious charge against Myles. We're not just on the Council together, we're also friends. Our fathers started this place together," he said.

"She's been outside with her mom so much, she doesn't know what she's saying," Kacy said, and sounded as if she were struggling for air as she said it. Kacy practically dragged Haze from the sitting position to her feet. "Anyway, it's been a long day. We need some sleep, especially if we have to get up with your little ones in the morning. I saw the extra blankets and that's what we need."

Haze hustled back to the room ahead of Kacy. The room contained two low-lying beds and multiple handmade blankets and rugs. Haze piled her blanket on top of her bed, which smelled of lavender and pine. Kacy picked up her blanket and unrolled it, snapping it through the air before bundling it across the bed.

"I don't know what you think you were doing. But you've just gotten yourself in trouble," Kacy said. "Did you hear what he said? He's going to report it to Myles."

"It's what I saw."

"Your family's out of here and you."

"Kacy—"

"I don't want to hear it. I'm going to sleep."

The wind moaned. The tree branches scratched against the window like a child that begging for attention.

Haze shifted in the bed, facing the door to watch if anyone entered. Kacy was already fast asleep. She slept so easily in a house with a male stranger. Haze kicked off the covers when someone's light footsteps padded past their door, stopping for a moment, as if listening and then continued on. Haze had been used to her father's footsteps and snores.

The Sisterhood had put them out and now the Freemen would do the same. Was there nowhere in this world that would accept them?

Haze remained buried under the covers until Kacy shook her roughly the next morning. "Lily or Amie's already up. Their kids will be up soon," she said.

Haze rolled over and Kacy gasped. Haze's eye felt somewhat sticky, and her vision was blocked in a way it hadn't been before she went to sleep. She pulled something gooey from over her eye.

"It's twice the size it was last night," Kacy said, and backed away. Haze wanted to scream that it wasn't her fault that this thing kept happening. "Your eye's been oozing something out of it."

Haze turned towards the window. "Go down first. I'll come down as soon as I clean up and fix my hair over it," she said.

She waited until Kacy was gone and then opened the window. Like at the Sisterhood, the windows were easy to climb in and out of. Haze hoisted herself up and jumped down into the shrubs. The sunlight hadn't punched through the sky yet.

She closed the window and headed north.

By the time she arrived at Millie's the sun had crested the horizon. She knocked on the door and when no one answered, she went towards the back and found Millie in her garden once again. She hadn't noticed the lemon tree in the corner the first time.

Millie didn't seem surprised to see her, but sighed at the sight of Haze's eye. "Back for a second round?" she asked, and rose, dusting off her overalls.

"I need something to make this thing go away," Haze said. Was Millie completely alone? No children or grandchildren? "I'll probably have to face the Council again today and I can't do it looking like this."

"You with the Council again?" Millie said, and Haze followed her inside her home. A small brown and white dog napped on a nearby cushion. "Have you done something against the Freemen? Stolen water or something?"

"No," Haze said, and her throat burned hot with fear. "I'm not a seer. Or at least I don't think that I am. But I keep having these visions."

Millie pulled out the three jars and continued searching for something else. "What kind of visions?"

"Of different things. I started having them right before Ty brought me here. I don't know what they mean. I don't know any of these men. I just know that something's wrong with the men. In one of my visions a man was dying in the field," Haze said, and threw up her hands and collapsed into the chair she'd sat in before. She hadn't noticed the bookcase tucked inside a foyer. There were no books, just more jars.

Millie filled a soot-covered pot with water and some herbs and placed it on the smoldering fireplace. "No one's died in the fields here, that I know of," she said.

Haze stopped at looked at the sweater she wore and said, "I left my jacket with the bottle still in it. Millie, what was in that bottle? It made me sick."

"That's what it was supposed to do," Millie said, stirring the concoction with a small stick and then using a metal rod to knock the ashes from the log. "The last thing the Council wants is a sick girl on their hands or one that passes out while being questioned."

Haze decided not to tell her she hadn't taken it in time. She said, "they're not going to let us stay. They're going to kick us out. Because I told Clint that Myles was lying."

"You're getting mighty worked up. Nothing's happened. I think that's why that caul of yours keeps growing."

"Cauls are for newborns," Haze said. "My brother was born with one."

"Then you must be birthing something," Millie said, and took the hot liquid from the fire and poured it into a cup. "Drink this down."

"What is that? What's it going to do to me?" Haze said, leaning away from the cup. She didn't want to faint again. Who knows who might find her next time? And they wouldn't be as kind as Ty.

"Remove that caul. Tonight. It might sting a little. Do what you can to stall out the Council until tomorrow. Give that skin time to come off."

Haze lifted the pungent-smelling cup to her lips and drank the sweet, syrupy liquid. "I hope this works," she said after draining the cup.

Millie set the cup aside. "Tell me all that was said."

Haze told her about the Council and the storm and her and Kacy staying overnight with Clint and his family. She left out the parts about Ty and passing out in the storm and Hugh. She clenched her teeth to keep from tearing up. "So, I left this morning before everyone saw me except Kacy," she said.

"I don't know the girl, but she's right. Your family will be thrown out. One thing the Sisterhood didn't teach you is that you should not share every detail with a man just because you can. You have to know when to keep your mouth shut. Your grandmother knows. That's why she made it through."

"Aren't the Freemen supposed to protect women and children?"

"That's their creed. But they're not going to do it for every woman. Especially for one that won't listen. Whatever vision you're having, either you live with it and make it work for you. Or you leave here and find another community. What you don't do is head out alone and stay alone."

Haze's eye stopped the awful itching. "How do you know about the Sisterhood?" she asked.

Millie's face softened and her lips twitched as she said, "I had a life before I came here and a husband or two. The Sisterhood has been around for a long time. The Destruction just made it harder for them to exist." She scooped up the cup and the pot from the now dead fire.

"Like Myles is making it hard for me? What kind of man does that?"

"Not all adult males are men," Millie said, and turned around with a fury, "Especially that one. Came around here more than once asking me for the same blue bottle I gave you and I told him no. He shouldn't be on the Council. He's not fit to lead. He couldn't even lead his own household without tampering with someone else's, and he's not fit to serve anyone either. He's polluted the Council since day one. Making rules to serve himself and no one else. So many of the men believe him because he says he's holy. He says that and not much else. Then they sit without wives and drink."

"I've known women without husbands and they don't drink."

"That you know of," Millie said. "In a woman, it can come out in a different way."

And something about the way she said it made Haze wonder if Myles did this because her mother wasn't married. Was Myles doing this to her because she didn't have a father?

Everyone in the Sisterhood had mothers and grandmothers and sometime aunties. When Haze had first showed up, she had talked about her father and cried for him. But the Sisterhood leaders allowed her to speak and then changed the subject until she learned not to speak about him. Now she'd found him and still couldn't speak about him.

Haze picked up a small silver knife from the counter. She almost saw her reflection in the shiny utensil and said, "I better get back. They probably know I'm not there."

Millie pried the knife from her hand. "And they know why. Remember what I said."

***

This time, Millie let Haze find her way out. Despite the sun, the sky remained a bleak gray. The syrupy taste of the concoction remained in the back of her throat, and Millie had given her some mint leaves to chew. Instead of heading back to Clint's home, Haze made a detour towards the bunkhouse.

In the bunkhouse down from her, the men were already hard at work on repairing the building. The silhouette of the men and the stomping of their feet as they ripped off and repaired a roof echoed through the area.

Her bunkhouse hadn't been touched yet. The roof had fallen in on the corner right over her bed. Some of the water had dried up, but the damp, swollen floor still had small pools of water. Haze found her cloth sack still inside the basket and mostly dry. She heaved it onto her back and a tiny beaded pouch fell out. She picked it up. It was the pouch that Shaye had given her the day she left the Sisterhood.

"I can't believe I still have this," she said, in a whisper that only the walls heard.

Haze opened it up, and Shaye had nestled a necklace and earrings inside and a little mirror. The Sisterhood had a few mirrors that the women had found over the years or brought with them when entering the Sisterhood.

Haze held up the mirror, which fit in her palm. The veil had created a slight hood over the outer corner of her eye.

"Haze?" Ty said from outside the window, and she nearly dropped the mirror.

What was he doing here? She didn't want to be seen like this by anyone.

Haze ducked down.

"Haze, come out of there."

CHAPTER 27

Ty tapped the wall outside, and it echoed inside. "You shouldn't be in there," he said.

Haze ruffled through the other women's baskets for anything she might need, but found nothing. No weapons, no water pouches, nothing.

Although Kacy had a single baby sock with the name Penny sewn into it, stashed at the bottom of her basket. Haze hoped that someone had put the other sock on Kacy's niece before burying the baby. She carefully put them back, took her sack and went outside. Ty, once again, wore the same dark gear of the guards. And this time, he had a gun strapped across his back.

Haze wanted to cover her face, but instead asked, "Why do you have that gun?"

"To protect the Freemen," he said, and deftly moved away as a piece of the roof fell into the grass near his feet. He'd had that gun when she first saw him, but she'd been so out of it that she hadn't remembered until now.

"Why do you have that knapsack?"

"So nobody will take it," Haze said and navigated so that he was on the good side of her face, and she could see him clearly. "Did something happen during the storm or last night?"

"Something always happens. That's why I have it."

He led her away from the bunkhouse and took a different path than the one Iris always used. "Was there something in that knapsack that you need? You're not supposed to be there."

"For a scarf or something to put over my eye. It wasn't like this when you found me. Ever since I've been here, this thing keeps growing."

He scrutinized her, including the veil. "Are you reacting to something? Several of the people here are allergic to certain plants or herbs. The Council has forbidden anyone to grow them."

"It started before you brought me here," Haze said. It had started while she was still in the Sisterhood but was so tiny, she had ignored it.

Ty stopped in his tracks. "Where are you staying? Should I take you west or north?"

Haze thought for a second. "Where does Iris live?"

"Closer to the south gate. She won't come this way today since she moved you. Why?"

Haze twirled a lock of her hair around her finger and then stopped. The Sisterhood had talked about those types of behaviors. Haze wasn't sure why she did it.

"I want to see where she lives, that's all. If it's as nice as Clint's or better than the bunkhouse," she said.

"This way."

Iris lived in a hillier area of the land. Ty nodded to another older guard that patrolled, and the man lit a smoke and never broke his stride. Haze kept her head turned in the opposite direction, as if studying the homes until the other guard passed.

"Ty, what happened that night with the fire?"

"Why do you ask these type of questions? Most that come here want to know what they will do every day and how they'll be fed."

Haze ducked under a branch. He asked this as if he didn't know that he brought her here with Hugh. "I don't understand the way things are. With the Council or how everyone's separated. The married people live on one side and everyone else on the other side."

"There were no married people where you lived before? Marriage isn't new. It was around before the Destruction."

"My parents were married, I think," Haze said, remembering Millie's words about keeping her mouth shut. Ty was a guard. He was one with the Council. She shouldn't trust him. Except he'd done nothing for her not to trust him. She sighed, leaving a white trail of breath in the air. "Have you met Iris's husband?"

"I've seen him," he said, leading her down a winding path until they came to a slope above a group of flat homes. "She lives down there."

Haze edged down the slope. It looked no different from the bunkhouses except for the small gardens in the back. The people had already left for the morning.

As if reading her thoughts, Ty said, "Many of them have been assigned to strengthen Millie's area. That's where the fire was, too. Someone set it on purpose."

"Someone inside?"

"Yes. When the Council finds out who did it, they'll be cast out," he said, and seemed to weigh his words before he spoke, "But you have visions. Do you know who did it?"

"No. But you said yesterday that you deal with reality. So why would you ask me about my visions? If I actually had them," she said, lifting her chin a little.

"Do you?"

Haze kicked the rocks in front of her and said, "Myles is going to get rid of my family because he thinks that I do."

"He and the Council have gotten rid of people for far less," Ty said, he kicked a rock the same time as her. The two rocks collided, and it knocked her rock sideways. "Like my father."

"What happened to him?"

"He's been missing for the last two quarters," he said. Haze shook her head in bewilderment. "Half a jubilee. He was also a guard but for the West gate. The Council's area. He patrolled the perimeter outside the gate one night. Like I did last night and many times before. No one has seen him after."

"Is that why you were so far from the Freemen when you found me?

"Yes. It rained hard in the days before and after his patrol. I couldn't track his steps. So if you're a seer, perhaps you can see what happened?" Ty asked, and there was a strain of hopefulness to his voice that Haze recognized.

"If you tell anyone this, I'll say you made it up. But the night before you brought me here, I saw a vision of three men fighting. I couldn't see their faces and didn't know who they were. But now I think it was the Council. I don't know if one of them was your father."

"Who won?

"I didn't see that."

"What else have you seen?"

"A man dying in the fields," Haze said, too afraid to mention Clint's baby. "He was much older than Clint."

"My father's younger and looks it."

"But that's not all. Last night, Iris took Kacy and me to Clint's home with his wives. And that's when I realized that Myles is working with someone against the Council."

Ty grabbed her by the arm and stopped her. "Did you see that in your vision?" Haze nodded and pulled her arm away. "Have you told anyone that?"

Haze fought to control herself against Ty's intensity. "Clint. And he said he had to report it. That's why I left this morning."

"You shouldn't have said that. Not to Clint, not to anyone," Ty said, pivoting as if he expected someone to follow them.

"Not even you?"

"I'm not the Council," he said and pulled her back towards the trees. "You should've told me this at the bunkhouse. They're probably looking for you right now."

"I need to tell my grandmother and mot—"

"Do you remember the three people that bunked with you the other day? Their bodies were found last night in the ravine not too far outside the gate. The rain washed away whatever dirt was covering them, but not the maggots."

Haze tasted the mint flowing back into her mouth along with the syrupy concoction. She turned away moments before it flew from her mouth.

Ty handed her a piece of cloth when she straightened up. She took it and, keeping her back to him, wiped her mouth. "My father's down there. He's married to Iris," she said.

"I know."

Haze whirled around and asked, "What? How did you know?

"Your father came here after Myles was appointed. Every guard here knows what the men, women, and children look like. You resemble your mother. Except for your crooked teeth," he said, and the corners of his mouth tilted up slightly. "But the Council wouldn't know. They don't talk to the people anymore. They don't eat with us at the celebrations like they used to."

"Is your mother alive, Ty?"

"No. She's gone," he said and steered her away from the slopes and moved at a fast clip back up the path.

"Where are you taking me?"

"To Millie."

"I just came from there."

"Then you need to go back," he said and steered her through a foliage-filled path.

For almost the entire way, they took the paths packed with trees and shrubs. They came upon Millie's again, but this time from the back end.

Millie wasn't in her yard.

Ty knocked on her door, and there was no answer, just the jangle of wind chimes.

"Are you staying with me? What am I supposed to do here?"

He opened the door and pushed her inside and said, "Stay out of sight. When Millie returns, tell her I brought you here."

Ty shut the door before Haze responded. She leaned her forehead against the door for a moment.

CHAPTER 28

At first, Haze stayed in the living space, and eventually, curiosity got the better of her, and she roamed around Millie's home.

The little dog trotted behind her, wagging its tail.

The home wasn't just filled with plants, but also quilts and some sort of pottery. Haze didn't go through any of the drawers. Who knows what Millie kept in them?

But she did snoop through the jars in the kitchen, none of which were labeled. And found dried Sassafras root, Flowering Dogwood, Sage, Coneflower and Sweetgrass among others.

Haze sneezed and quickly replaced the lids. She ran her finger across the handcrafted tables. Yes, the Freemen stayed busy building things. She hunkered down on the rug and scratched the little dog behind his ears.

If only she could pick up a few members of the Sisterhood and move them here, like Shaye, who knew what was important about life.

Wait—the Sisterhood said that, but so did Myles. Could those two women in her vision be from the Sisterhood? Haze shook her head. No, the Sisterhood was several weeks' trek away.

Haze went around the house again, this time with more care, searching for any sign of the Sisterhood's way of maintaining a home.

Was someone shouting? A vision rolled like thick mud in front of her. It was those men again, with the women, exchanging sacks outside the gate. Except there was another man, watching them from behind a nearby tree. The man didn't make a sound.

But someone was shouting. Millie's voice mingled with the voice of Iris grew louder as they approached the door. Haze ran into the foyer and hid. It sounded as if Iris came through the door first. She shooed away Millie's little dog, who ran to the door barking when Millie entered with Iris.

"I'm not going to repeat myself. I saw her this morning. Gave her something for her eye, and she left."

"Did she say where she was going?"

"No. And I didn't ask her," Millie said, and then nudged her barking dog, "Buster, sit."

"Millie, it's important that we find her. She's been missing all morning."

"I expect so," Millie said and placed her hands on her hips. "You and the rest of them scared her half to death. She's probably scaled the wall already."

"Her mother's still here, as is her grandmother."

"The Council's not after them. Buster, be quiet!"

Haze peeked out from the foyer and Iris stood right where she'd been minutes ago. Millie faced the door with her back to Haze. Buster ran back over to the foyer, wagging his tail.

"They need to speak with her right away," Iris said, and her shadow moved across the floor.

"You said that already. But if you need time to nose around my house, go ahead," Millie said, digging into her pocket and pulling out a small treat. "Good boy. Let's get you something to eat."

Buster trampled over Iris's feet and ran to Millie.

Iris jerked away as if she'd been slapped, "If you see her—"

"I'll not have anything to do with it. You can tell the Council I said that."

The door clicked behind Iris, and Millie took one of the jars from the windowsill and shook the contents into Buster's bowl. And poured a bit of water into the second bowl and placed it by the door. "How long do you plan to hide back there?" she asked.

Haze slowly came from the foyer and sank into the chair. She put her head down on the table.

"Go on and have a good cry," Millie said. "Get it out of your system so you can think clearly."

"I don't cry," Haze said, swallowing against the lump in her throat. What good would it do? Some of the Sisterhood had punished her the two times she had cried while there. Anytime her mother saw Haze's tears years ago, she'd sent her to set traps of find water. "Ty brought me here."

Millie went to window, and Haze followed her.

Iris had already disappeared up the path.

"Then what do you need from me?" Millie asked, and carefully brushed the locks from

Haze lowered her head, letting the bang drop back over her eye, and said, "To stay here until Ty gets back."

CHAPTER 29

When night fell and the few birds that dared the cold stopped chirping, Haze gathered her sack. She picked up one of the glass jars and shook it. And caught a whiff of dried dandelions. She could learn a lot from Millie. And she would have.

Haze set the jar down with a thump.

Millie shook her head and said, "You need to stay until Ty returns."

"I can't," Haze said, stuffing Millie's provisions of dried meat and herbs into her sack. "I don't know what they've done with my family. I have to protect them."

"You have that backwards. It's their job to protect you."

The throbbing in Haze's eye flared. "That's not how it works. Not for me," she said, touching the soft eye patch that Mille had made before stuffing it into her knapsack. Haze had used the beads from Shaye's pouch to embroider it. Haze hugged Millie and said, "I wish you had lived in the Sisterhood."

Millie left the lanterns lit in the living space, put out the ones in the kitchen, and said, "And I wish you would stay put. You've been on your own long enough already."

Haze went out the back door and followed the path that Ty had used earlier. Millie had told her how to get to the south gate and how to get to her mother and grandmother on the visitor's quarter side.

Haze headed in the direction of the south gate side and stuck to the shadows. Every rustle of the shrubs or the grass made her check over shoulder. She paused every so often and made sure no guards patrolled in each space she went into, or the place didn't have a lot of lanterns.

When the visitor's quarters were in sight, Haze hid by a row of shrubs and sat watching the place until she stiffened with cold.

Finally, Walker came outside and lit a smoke.

Her mother had no reason to come outside if she was still there. Haze didn't dare stir Walker's attention. There had to be another way. Still on the outskirts, she circled around the quarters and hoped Kacy had returned.

Haze drew as close as she dared and peeked through the window nearest the woman's space. Fran and Irma were talking. If Kacy was there, Haze couldn't see her. She angled to the corner of the window and her grandmother was in bed, but her mother wasn't there.

"She's gone."

Haze jumped, and Walker continued leaning on the corner of the building with his smoke.

"The guards took her earlier," he said, flicking the smoke onto the ground and grinding it out. "You'd better get out of here. I knew you was trouble from day one. I guess it ain't sank in for Ty yet."

"Where is he?"

"Don't know. Don't know where Kacy is either. They didn't come by looking for her, though. Just you. Whatever you did, you need to get outta here. 'Cause they're coming for you. They gave orders for everyone to stay inside."

A long dog howl shattered the moment of silence. A faint memory of the Sisterhood's stories about dogs hunting people made Haze back away.

She bolted into the darkness and ran until her lungs ached.

Where could she go? Back over the wall into the forest alone? And get lost in the Deadwoods?

Haze ran for several minutes, straining to run faster with each step. When she reached the gate, she discovered there were twice as many guards as before. She needed a ladder to get over the wall. She went along the edges, checking for tunnels underneath the wall, and found none.

The dogs' barks grew closer, tearing through the silence as they raced towards the gate. The largest dog charged her, and Haze screamed as the dog leaped towards her.

It hit the wall right where she'd stood and fell to the ground, stunned.

But another dog sprang from the darkness.

Haze swung a thick branch at the animal and screamed, "Help! HELP."

The dog caught the branch in its teeth and ripped it from her grip.

Three guards rushed from the guard station.

The snarling dog suddenly turned, wagging its tail at some unheard-by-a-human sound.

Haze ran behind the first guard, still screaming.

The second guard took the dog by the collar and wrenched it away from everyone.

"It's the girl with the eye sore," the first guard said and exchanged looks with the third guard, who quickly disappeared out the station door. The first guard, Trent, was the same one Haze had seen the night of the barbeque when she had tried to sneak away with Hugh.

The second guard patted the dog and said, "She's nothing but trouble from what I've heard. Return her to the outside. Let her go."

"Can't," Trent said and jerked Haze from behind him as if she were a weed pulled from the ground. "Calm down. You're all right,"

Haze held onto her sack, her body shaking from her deep ragged breaths. No blood on her clothes. She didn't have any bite marks on her. The other guards in the station went about their routine as if she weren't there. She wanted to ask for Ty but didn't want to get him in trouble, too. Trent guided her over to a chair.

"Can I have some water?" she asked and something wet almost seeped out of her eye. Haze held it back. No, she wouldn't cry.

"Here you go," Trent said and held the glass out and seemed immune to Haze's shaking hands.

No one said anything else to her, and she didn't have to wait long. When the third guard entered the station, he held the door open, and Myles entered.

CHAPTER 30

Myles' mouth briefly curled into a smile and then he pasted on a disappointed expression. The guards stood back in the small room and Myles slowly made his way over to her. "So, you've chosen to accuse me of going against the Council and then decided to escape your words?"

Haze backed up as if she'd been kicked in the gut. "You said my family and I were free to go. So, I wasn't escaping. I was out walking, like I've done before until I was chased by dogs. I thought those dogs would tear me apart. And they almost did. Why am I here like this? Can't I speak to Clint and Wes?" she asked.

Myles picked up her lock and studied the small beads woven into it and said, "They've already decided. That's why I'm here." He had a jaw the shape of a lantern and a giant vein pulsed as he spoke. "In the Freemen society, we don't accuse other people of wrongdoing and expect to walk away. And since you're a seer, it is you that should've seen this coming. You are under arrest," he said, and turned to the guards. "Take her to the lockhouse."

The lockhouse resembled the bunkhouse and the visitor quarters, without windows and a door that locked from the outside only. The lantern was outside the door as well. Haze spent hours curled on the stiff bed.

Haze wasn't trying to sleep and couldn't sit still. She dragged her hands across her face and tried the locked door for the umpteenth time, as if she expected it to unlock if she twisted the knob enough.

She threw herself back onto the bed.

She should've stayed at Millie's and waited for Ty. Or went near Clint's home and hid. Or maybe her father's home.

Haze drew her knees up to her chest. Did they do something to her mother? Or Kacy when they found her gone?

The guards had kept her knapsack. But she still had her small, beaded pouch and rubbed it in the darkness.

The knob twisted and a door knock. "Haze, it's me," her father said.

Haze's heart leaped into her throat. The door opened, and he came in with the lantern. Haze sat up wondering what he wanted and who told him she was here. Myles? Ty?

"Hey," he said awkwardly and turned around, unsure of where to sit. "I'll bet you weren't expecting me."

"What are you doing here?"

"I was sent. Can't say by who. Well, when I found out, I wanted to come. Actually," he cracked his knuckles one-by-one. "Listen. You're in trouble, and I'm here to help."

"Why?"

"Because you need help," he said, and folded himself into the chair across from her.

"Are they going to kill me?"

His head jerked up. "No."

"Then why am I in here? Where's my mother?"

"I don't know about your mother. I'm not here for that."

The icy feeling of dread ballooned in her belly. "Are you going to get me out of here? Can I leave with you?"

"Tell me. I want you to tell me about these visions you have. The one where one Council member has allies with others outside the Council," he said.

Haze understood. Clint had sent him. But that meant nothing because Clint agreed to lock her up. He reached out and patted her on the knee as if she were still the eight-year-old that he'd left behind.

The lantern illuminated the flash of his wedding band.

"Why are you here? Why should I tell you anything? Where's my mother? Did they put her out?" Haze asked and rose from the bed. "You saw me yesterday, and you didn't speak. Not one word. Now you have all these questions? No.

Unless I know my mother's okay, I'm not answering Clint's or whoever's questions."

Her father went to the door and said, "She wants her mother."

Haze wanted to run to the door, but he was blocking it. Over his shoulder, three guards waited with her mother. Once they let go of her mother, she hurried into the lockhouse and enveloped Haze in a hug.

"Are you hurt? Let me look at you," her mother said and ran her hands over Haze as if expecting Haze to have holes somewhere on her body.

Her father cleared his throat. "We need answers, or they won't let her go," he said. Her mother stepped to the side as if she'd never seen him before and swept him from his feet to his head. Finally, her gaze settled on his wedding band.

She turned her back on him and said to Haze, "Talk to me."

"I already told you about the seer stuff. Myles is against the Council. He's just faking it. I had a vision and saw five men outside the gate with two women."

"What men? What did they look like? Tall and thin? Short and stocky?" her father asked.

"Men are good at pretending," her mother said.

Her parents stared at one another over Haze's head.

"They're going to attack this place," Haze said, finally saying the words out loud.

"Who?" her father asked.

"I don't know who. But they will. Myles paid for it somehow."

"Did you see when it would happen?" he asked.

"My visions don't work like that. I don't know how they work. I don't know anything," Haze said, waving her hands in the air as if to bat away their questions. "Who sent you both here?"

"Clint," her mother said.

Her father said, "Same."

The guards opened the door and pushed their way inside. "You've had enough time. Let's hear it."

These were a different set of guards than the ones she'd been with earlier. And still no Ty. Haze immediately said, "I didn't tell them anything. There's nothing to tell. Why don't you just let me and my mother go?"

"How about we bring your brother in here, and you can all have a Freemen family reunion?" the guard asked.

"What?" her mother said, pushing Haze away from the door and the guards. "Don't you think about bringing my son here."

Her father went back to popping his knuckles again. "What's his name?"

"Hugh," her mother said coolly.

"I'll go get him," said the second guard.

"Don't you dare!" her mother said. "He's too young to go through this."

So am I, Haze wanted to say. Both her parents wanted answers from her, but neither protested that she had to go through this, and neither cared what she went through in the Deadwoods.

"Haze," her father said. "Repeat what you said. Let's end this for them."

Her mother said, "Haze, you can't let them put Hugh in here. You have to save your brother." She shook Haze a little as if Haze had been sleeping and needed to wake up.

Haze dropped the little pouch still in her hand. For the longest time, she had waited to see both her parents together. But this wasn't how she'd imagined it. The wetness seeped from her bad eye again.

"I made it up. I've been making this up the whole time. I don't see anything. I promise I don't," Haze said. The icy feeling in her belly had moved up to her throat. She had tried to hide, to run away, and still failed. This veil had created nothing but problems for her. If only boys were seers with the Freemen, then so be it. "You can tell Myles that I was lying. I'm not a seer. Just let me go."

CHAPTER 31

The guards put their guns back into their waistbands. Haze pushed away from all of them. She just wanted to run away from these people. Run to somewhere that she wasn't punished just for showing up. Her father did it. Why not her?

Her father placed his arms loosely around her. It reminded her of how Phoenix used to hug her. It looked warm and loving. "You're scaring my daughter," he said.

"Why didn't you bring your daughter when you first showed up here? I didn't know you had one," the first guard said. "Or a son."

"Now you do."

"We have our orders, and you know that. From the same person that sent you here," the second guard said. "Ollie too, and Roy."

Haze squinted at him, wondering if he was one of the five men from her vision. "Who sent you?" she asked, and neither guard answered. This couldn't have started when she showed up. Not the way that Ty had spoken about Myles. Myles had to have been this way all along. Ty must believe that Myles had those three people killed and maybe his father.

"Your daughter's a plant here. Someone put her here, and that's when all of these fires started. This isn't the kind of girl we need here. Ty needs to answer for this," the second guard said.

Her parents awkwardly shifted from foot to foot.

"She's not a seer or whatever the Council thinks," her father said. "Let her go. If you want her to leave the Freemen, then she will, her and her mother," he said.

For a moment, Haze stopped struggling. Her and her mother returning to struggle through life in the Deadwoods was of no consequence to him.

The Sisterhood putting them out had been of no consequence to the women there after she spent the spring helping them build—firepits and cabinets, and plant for the coming harvest until her nails and hands cracked from the work.

A loud thump across the lockhouse roof made everyone look up. One of the guards outside the lockhouse yelled, "What was that?"

A second thump followed, but this time no sound from the guards outside. Haze and her parents moved back from the door into the furthest corner of the small, windowless room. Haze's father blew out the lantern. The two guards, guns drawn, quickly opened the door, and no one was there.

Haze's stomach felt as shaky as a bowl of soup.

The second guard didn't have time to fire his weapon because a man jumped from either side of the door and tried to grab the guards' guns.

The gun went off, and the first guard thudded to the floor. The second guard fired on both men, and one guard ducked back outside the house.

Her father pushed her to the floor, and Haze scrambled under the bed. From the floor, the guard's unseeing eyes stared at her in the dim light. Haze put the beaded pouch in her mouth and bit down on it to keep from screaming. Her mother's screams bounced off the walls.

Her father grabbed the chair and swung it at the first man, which knocked him onto the bed. The man grabbed at her father as he fell and landed on the bed with a loud grunt. The men struggled on the bed, pinning Haze underneath it. The second guard yelled, "Move out the way."

"My daughter's under there," her mother shrieked. But his gun jammed.

Haze tried to wiggle out, but the weight of the two men above pressed down on her. Her mother grabbed her by the rope between her wrists and dragged her from underneath. The men rammed against the wall and overturned the bed.

Haze sniffed the air. The lantern didn't make that smell. "Something's burning," she said, pulling her mother to the door.

The guard fired towards the ceiling, and when her father heard the popping sounds, he tried to push the man away.

Haze looped her arm through her mother's and opened the door. Ty ran up the path.

"Ty, they're in here."

"Get out of there," Ty said.

Haze and her mother ran down the path, and when she turned, half of the roof was on fire, and pieces fell into the grass. In the distance, another fire rose above treetops and the dog howls rose even higher than the fire. Haze wasn't sure, but the fire seemed to be over near Millie's area again.

Ty ran past them and kicked open the door to the house.

The piercing siren from the day before went off and rattled Haze. The wind chilled her to the bone while the orange blaze licked the night sky.

"Don't let that fire be at the children's quarters," her mother said

Her mother's words chilled her more than the wind. The fire ate up the corner of the roof and spread to the middle.

A gun blast replaced the popping sounds Haze had heard before and she and her mother hid behind a tree.

"Should we go back to the Sanctuary?" her mother asked.

The shrubs surrounding them rustled, and Hal emerged from the foliage. Like Ty had earlier, he had his gun strapped to his back. "That's the first place they'll look. Your daughter's coming with me."

"Going with you where?" her mother asked, dragging Haze away from him and further away from the burning lockhouse.

Her father staggered from the lockhouse with Ty and the other guard, and smoke poured out the door behind them. They coughed and took a few moments to catch their breath.

"Listen, I have orders to get her," Hal said, latching his fingers between the thin rope around Haze's wrists and pulling her towards him.

"Orders from who?" her mother asked, her voice rising faster than the blaze. Black smoke curled over all the hissing and crackling flames. "You're not taking my daughter anywhere without me. You'll have to come through me. You can tell that to the Council. I'll give my life for my children!"

"Not your concern," Hal said and pulled a small knife from his waistband and cut the rope around her wrist. Haze shook her hands free, and Hal put the cut rope into his pocket. "Someone is in here destroying the place again." He turned to Haze's father. "I'll take your daughter with me if you don't mind."

Haze's hand flew to her mouth in horror, and she quickly put it down. "He doesn't."

She had told the guards about an attack, but she hadn't expected it to happen so soon. Without waiting for their words or looking back, Ty and Hal guided Haze back to the path towards the east part of the base.

"I'm going back to Clint's?" she asked.

"You're going to my place. Millie will meet you there," Hal said.

Haze didn't know how much Clint had told Hal, so she didn't say anything. In the darkness, she still paid attention to the twists and turns that Hal took and also kept an eye on the position of the stars and the moon.

She didn't get the chance to ask her mother where she stayed. She wondered what her parents would say to one another once she'd left. If they said anything at all. The smell of the smoke layered the air, and Hal hurried her along.

"I need to get you inside before that siren wakes up every soul. It's just a bunch of us guards here," Hal said, and like Ty earlier that day, he took her in the back entrance to his house. "Don't speak," he said, picking up one of the lanterns in the yard. He steered her to the first room adjacent to the entrance, and Haze tiptoed the entire time.

Once Hal closed his bedroom door, he said, "You're just going to stay in here. No one ever comes in this room. They're too used to me checking on them when I'm home. But you need to stay hidden and stay still."

Hal put her inside the closet and left, and Haze waited, afraid to make a sound. The siren went off again and screamed for several minutes, and Haze plugged her ears. Hal didn't live alone. The floor had light vibrations from at least two people moving around in another part of the house.

She heard the door creak open, and she quickly moved behind some old pants hanging in the front of the closet. But that wasn't all. Haze silently wedged open the trap living space that Hal had showed her, prepared to scoot down under the house.

The cat quiet footsteps went around the room and Haze shimmed into the hole. The footsteps came to a stop in front of the closet living space, and it creaked open as Haze pulled the trap living space shut above her head.

CHAPTER 32

The footsteps entered the closet while Haze made her way under the house. From her spot, she worked her way towards the glow from the lanterns in the backyard. A bigger glow came from the fires, which had grown and silhouetted the sky along with the thickening smoke. Haze placed her hand over her mouth and nose and tried not to cough.

There was a loud thud from the spot above her and a crash as two men slammed through the living space and rolled down the steps.

Haze froze.

The men wrestled with one another on the ground, and the thud she'd heard was the men's punches to one another.

The first man wore guard gear. Haze recognized him as Barney, the one along with the female guard that had turned her away from the gate days ago. The second man was Ollie, who was about 20 years older than Barney and closer to Hal's age.

Barney had Ollie on his back and Ollie kicked Barney backwards so that he fell against the steps.

Ollie rose to his feet and charged at him. Another blow and another one, and Haze wanted to plug her ears.

Barney said, "You brought her here. You and him."

Another pair of footsteps thudded above, followed by a third man's voice, "She's not in here."

It was Roy.

The men coughed through the smoke.

Ollie flung Barney onto the steps. "Shoot him," Barney screamed, followed by a popping sound.

Haze held in her scream and her coughing as Ollie's body fell to the ground.

"Search it again. She's in there somewhere. I saw Hal bring her here," Roy said.

Haze stayed under the steps and waited until the men's footsteps faded back into the house. The smoke had thickened even more, and when it and the clouds shaded the moon,

Haze wriggled from under the house and checked that no one was in the doorway, and she bolted down the path.

Roy had a fit of coughing and said, "There she is. Get her."

In the Sisterhood, Haze had been one of the fastest girls, but her time inside the Freemen's gates with Ty, Walker, and Reed had shown her true speed.

Barney would catch her.

Haze didn't dare scream and couldn't if she wanted to. She barely saw through the smoke in front of her and that meant that Barney and Roy wouldn't see as well either.

Footsteps pounded down the path after her.

Haze zigzagged through the shrubs. No, she wasn't going to outrun them.

She dipped behind a tree and heard one pair of footsteps run by.

She hunched down behind the tree.

The leaves on the ground crackled about five feet away. She stayed down and clapped her hand over her mouth. Her throat itched, and she struggled to breathe.

A small cough told her that Roy was to her left.

Haze carefully stepped over the dead leaves and crawled to the other side of a shrub to her right. Her heart pounded so hard that Haze was sure the man might hear it.

"The fire's coming this way," Roy shouted, and Barney sprinted away, although he'd been so close that Haze smelled the foot order from his boots.

The faint shouts of the people working to put out the fire grew louder.

Haze coughed uncontrollably and half-rolled out from under the shrub.

The crackling and hissing sound grew louder, and the faint orange glow was no longer faint. When she stood, the smoke filled her lungs.

She ran in the direction that had no orange glow, tripping twice, until finally she drew breath without as much smoke. The trees thinned, and she found herself in another area with two or three bunkhouses lining the path.

Two women were already on the path with small children, walking them back and forth to calm them down.

The first woman said, "Were you in that fire?"

"Yes," Haze said, adjusting her hair over her eye and hoping that the women hadn't heard about her.

"How bad is it over there?" the first woman asked.

"It's scary," Haze said. "The guards are fighting to stop it."

The second woman pat the back of the child she held in her arms and asked, "Why were you there? That's the guards' job."

Haze shrugged. "I just wanted to see what was going on."

Without too much hurry, she went in the opposite direction. Once she was no longer in the women's line of sight, she circled back towards their path from a different angle.

The only places she knew besides the bunkhouse were Millie's or Clint's home.

CHAPTER 33

Haze crept to the back of Clint's house, hiding out by the water barrel. Clint had sent those men after her, and this would be the last place they'd look. She couldn't go to Millie's and Iris was out of the question since the Council knew that her father was there.

So what other options did she have?

Haze waited for an opportunity to get out of the cold. The lanterns lit up the inside of their home and Amie paced back and forth with Nyomi in her arms. Lily was also there, but Clint wasn't in the room.

The fire hadn't touched this side of the community at all except for a thin layer of smoke curling around the homes. The people in many of the homes were up and awake. A crowd of people gathered down the path and spoke in hushed tones, periodically stopping to point at the fire.

Haze lifted the water barrel top, drank her fill of water, and heard the click of the door opening. She pressed herself into the shadows, silently cursing for being so desperate.

It was Lily, with a pitcher in hand. She started to lift the top and then stopped, examining how the top that Haze had hastily returned. Lily went out a few feet, watching the crowd, and looked thoughtfully back at the barrel.

"Helllllooo," Lily shouted, waving her arms in the air. Haze groaned inwardly. "Does anyone need any water?" Before she finished her sentence, a handful of people came into the space. Lily dipped into the house and quickly returned with tin cups that they filled and drank like babies.

One stocky man asked, "What's Clint up to? How is he going to stop this? It's the second time in a week." He gulped down another cup of water.

The woman next to him said, "I'm scared. I heard that there were a bunch of strangers wandering around here causing trouble. We're supposed to be safe here."

"And you are, Deena," Lily said. "My husband will make sure of that."

"I know Myles and Wes are his buddies," the stocky man said, "But this has got to stop. Things have to return to normal. I shouldn't need a pass at night."

The door from the front of the house slammed and there was a rush of movement inside the house. From her angle in the shadows, Haze couldn't see who had entered the living space. But Amie's baby woke up and started crying.

"Has that been brought before the Council?" Deena asked and shoved the cup at Lily so that she tottered backwards.

"I have to get back inside," Lily said. "I wanted to make sure everyone had some water during this long night."

And the people grumbled as they left.

Lily replaced the water barrel top again and gave it a good shove to seal it. "Clint never reported it," she said, keeping her back to where Haze hid. Haze sucked in her breath. "It was Amie. Wes is her brother."

"Some men came after me tonight."

"Are you injured?"

"Not too much."

"Go to the room I had you in and stay there," Lily said. "Can you do that?"

"Yes," Haze said.

When Lily went back inside and blew out the lanterns by the door, that was the signal and Haze eased from shadow to shadow until she got to that window and climbed inside. Haze made a beeline for the blankets, needing to shake off the cold.

"You're back," Kacy said with a hiss. Haze hadn't seen her and jerked back, ready to dive back through the window. "Where have you been?"

Chapter 34

Haze opened her mouth to speak, and no words came out for several seconds. Finally, she said, "I tried, I tried to get away because Clint was going to tell Myles what I said. And Myles won't leave me alone."

"Myles was here earlier. Three or four times. I heard him and Wes and Clint fighting. Amie was crying for a long time. They left, though, and I haven't heard anything else. I'd heard enough anyway," Kacy said in barely a whisper.

Haze told her what had happened while the shouting in the living space grew louder and louder. Haze cracked the door open and caught the tail end of Amie's words, "I can't believe Hal's dead. That man was a guard when I was still Ty's age."

"We need to find that girl. She was the last one with him," another man said.

Haze closed the door. That could be one of the men that chased her tonight. She didn't get a chance to thank Hal for protecting her, and now she never would.

Clint said with a roar that made Kacy jump, "That girl has nothing to do with it. Get back out there. Find the men that did this. Or else Hal won't be the only one buried in the morning."

"Hey, they took your jacket this morning," Kacy said. "Plus, whatever was in that bottle."

"It was something for my eye," Haze said. The silence from the living space was even worse than the shouting.

"That's what I told'em," she said, lowering her voice even more and then fell silent at the footsteps outside the door.

Lily opened the door and Haze hid behind it. "Kacy, just checking if you want any water or anything," she said. "We have a lot going on out here and you've been in here a while."

Clint sidestepped his wife and pushed the door open. "You answered this already. But I have to ask again. Did Haze tell you anything about Myles? What he planned? Anything?"

Haze came from behind the door and said, "I told Kacy nothing. I told you the truth. And for that, Myles has been hunting me all day and all night."

"You've been here all this time?" Clint asked, his voice an uneven mixture of fury and disbelief.

"I told her to come inside a few minutes ago," Lily said, quietly.

"Clint?" Amie shouted. "The guards are here."

Haze wrapped the blanket tighter around herself and, to her own surprise, followed Clint and Lily back into the living space. Kacy trailed after them.

"Oh no. Not Trent," Kacy muttered under her breath.

Trent's face hardened with rage at Haze, and he said, "Wes is dead."

"What?" Amie said and clutched the baby to her. "Not Wes?"

"Yes," Trent said without an ounce of sadness.

"What happened?" Amie asked.

"We don't know yet," Trent said.

Half of the guards didn't move, and the other half looked uncertain before they finally moved towards Haze.

Clint raised his arm and said, "Leave her. Find Myles. Hal is dead."

"And Ollie," Haze said. "Roy and Barney did it."

"First Wes, now Hal and Ollie?" one of the other guards asked, pushing Trent aside.

Haze closed her eyes at those words. What kind of seer was she? She hadn't envisioned this happening.

"Please no. Not my brother. This has to be a mistake," Amie said and burst into crying like a water-filled cloud. "Wes is dead? He can't be dead. It makes no sense."

Amie held Nyomi, crying into the baby's blanket.

"We found him, and he's full of holes," Trent said.

Kacy put an arm around Amie's shoulder and said, "He was the first one to say I could stay here again."

"Why was he killed? Who did it?" Clint asked.

"Myles was the last one with him," the other guard said.

"Myles was here earlier," Lily said. "We told him we needed to speak with him and Wes. But it could wait until morning."

"Exactly! So why would Myles hurt Wes?" Amie screamed.

"Find Myles and arrest him," Clint said. "Take him to the lockhouse until morning."

Haze was still in stuck on the guard's words that Wes had been killed when Trent said, "We can't arrest Myles. He's gone. He went to the kid's quarters and took one of the boys too. That new one."

"Hugh?" Haze asked and it felt like the floor tilt beneath her feet. She couldn't catch her breath and the words came out in a whisper. "Myles took Hugh? Where's he taking him?"

"Don't know him," Trent said.

Lily said, "Haze, in the morning, we'll find him. Clint will have a plan. Just wait."

Haze waited with Lily and Kacy, silent in the living space while Clint comforted Amie. What did Myles want with Hugh? Where were her parents to protect Hugh?

***

When dawn broke, Haze and Kacy accompanied Clint to the firey spot. The sun and wind slowly cleared the smoke, yet wisps of it hung over every inch of the north and south gate areas.

As they approached the burnt bunkhouses, the bodies of the guards lined the path and, after that, the residents. Hal's body was at the beginning of the line. Five men, three boys, and one girl lay side-by-side on the sooty, brown grass.

Haze clapped her hands over her mouth, struggled not to wretch at the sight of the bodies, and turned away.

Kacy tapped her on the shoulder and pointed at the end of the line. Ty, his face streaked with soot, covered the children with a blanket.

"Ty," Haze said. She hurried over, hugging him longer than she had expected, and gently took a corner of the blanket and pulled it over the children. "I thought you – I don't know. I thought maybe they'd gotten you, too."

"Almost happened. They got the jump on Hal, though," he said, taking off his jacket and kneeling and covered Hal's face with it.

"I'm sorry, Hal," she said, even though he couldn't hear her. "He hid me. In his room. Barney and Roy couldn't find me."

"Actually, that's my room," Ty said. "There hadn't been much in it but the bed and clothes. "My dad built ...that."

Clint stood in front of the growing crowd of people and said, "Listen, Freemen, we will rebuild this community."

"Myles took Hugh last night," she said, ignoring the roar of approval from the crowd.

"I know."

"Ty, I have to find them," she turned away from the sight of Amie sobbing under a half-scorched tree. "I can't let anything happen to him. I'm supposed to protect him. Clint said he'd help, but he's got all of this happening right now. Can you come with me?"

Excerpt from Book 2: BEYOND THE DEADWOODS

Book 2: Beyond the Deadwoods

The afternoon turned colder than Haze expected. The only thing stiffer than the throbbing veil of skin over her eye was her hands. She rubbed her stiff fingers together and waited inside the small room hidden behind the North-gate for Clint and Ty to show up.

Trent was already there and Haze avoided him.

The other guards present, including the woman guard avoided Haze, too. They discussed the fire from the night before in hushed tones.

"It was an insider," the woman guard whispered. But after skimming over her shoulder at Haze waiting nearby, she fell silent.

Inside the small space, Haze couldn't ignore Hal's empty chair. She never got the chance to thank him. Although, she couldn't believe that he had hidden her in Ty's room. And Ty's room was clean.

The Sisterhood had told her that males lived like half-trained animals and their rooms smelled like a zoo. That's the one thing her grandmother had often agreed on and laughed about after sighing out Haze's grandfather's name.

Haze turned the vision she'd had earlier over in her mind once again. What was it about? She never recognized any of these people. She hadn't had the chance to tell her mother about them or her grandmother.

Only Ty.

She had no reason to trust him. Or any of the Freemen for that matter.

She tucked the small pouch she still had hidden under her clothes even further down into her scratchy pants. Don't trust the men, the Sisterhood told them. But her mother had trusted the Sisterhood, and they had put them out.

A rustle of noise announced Clint's arrival. Ty carried a large, black knapsack studded with six pockets on his back. He carried another in front of him, which he took off and tossed to Trent. Not far behind them, Kacy glided towards the Northgate. And not just her, but Walker too.

The community had been quiet since morning. No one worked the fields. Everyone secluded themselves in their homes or bunkhouses. Haze hadn't expected her parents to go with her, but at least one of them could see her off.

Ty actually had a third, smaller knapsack, which had been hidden behind his bag. He removed the smaller sack and handed it to Haze.

"Whaaaa," she squealed when it nearly pulled her to the floor.

"Let me," Ty said, retrieving it and helping put it on her back.

When Kacy and Walker reached them, they already had smaller knapsacks too.

"What's in these things?" Haze asked Clint.

"Food, water, and shelter," Trent grunted out.

Haze already wished they would leave him behind. He was one of Myles' pets. Didn't Clint know that? Ty? She wanted to say something, but with Myles already gone half the day, she didn't have time to alert the men to their mistake.

"My mother—" Haze said.

"Is with your grandmother," Clint said. "Kacy has something to share."

"Here to see me off?" Haze asked Kacy and hugged her. A small weight lifted off of Haze for just a moment. The Sisterhood always said it was best to go in pairs.

"I changed my mind," Kacy said, and once again, she examined Haze's hair and the small jewels woven into it. "Walker volunteered to come with us."

"I've never been outta the forest. I hear there's places full of nothing but girls," Walker said with a wink.

Kacy elbowed him.

Walker continued, "Girls that need my protection."

"Clint, where would Myles take Hugh?" Haze asked. Her brother's life was at stake and Walker had other plans. But who knew how helpful he might be. Outside the guards cranked the gate open.

Clint instructed them on the best route, one that would take them through the forest but avoid the Deadwoods.

About the Author

LATISHA REDDING is the author of the young adult novels, *In the Shadow of the Deadwoods*, and the sequel, *Beyond the Deadwoods*, along with the middle-grade novel *Leelee the Imposter* and her picture book series *Arrow's Great Escape From School* and *Arrow's Great Escape From Camp* and her debut picture book *Calling the Water Drum*. LaTisha attributes her love of storytelling to her parents gifting her with a book every Friday when she was young. And, she learned early on how good stories can illuminate even the darkest corners of life. LaTisha lives in the south and writes to shine a little light into those shadowy corners, reminding readers that even in the toughest times, there's always a story waiting to help us find our way. Visit her at: **www.latisharedding.com**

Also By